D1610336

couples, passersby

COUPLES, PASSERSBY

Botho Strauss

Translated by Roslyn Theobald

Northwestern University Press

Evanston, Illinois

Hydra Books
Northwestern University Press
Evanston, Illinois 60208-4210

The publisher gratefully acknowledges the financial assistance of
Inter Nationes, Bonn.

First published in German as
Paare, Passanten by Carl Hanser Verlag, Munich.

Published 1996 by Hydra Books/Northwestern University Press.

Printed in the United States of America
ISBN 0-8101-1242-6
Library of Congress Cataloging-in-Publication Data
Strauss, Botho, 1944-
[Paare, Passanten. English]
Couples, passersby / Botho Strauss ; translated by Roslyn Theobald.
p. cm.
ISBN 0-8101-1242-6 (alk. paper)
I. Theobald, Roslyn. II. Title.
PT2681.T6898P3313 1996
833'.914—dc20
96-31646
CIP

The paper used in this publication meets the
minimum requirements of the American National Standard
for Information Sciences—Permanence of Paper for
Printed Library Materials,
ANSI Z39.48-1984.

for dieter sturm

contents

couples

A man in a gray suit too short to fit is sitting alone at a table in a restaurant, and suddenly goes "Psst!" at the murmuring crowd, so loudly that after he repeats it two more times the swell of voices is lulled, almost seeping away, and everyone is looking his way by the time a last powerful "Psst!" finally gives way to deathly silence. The man raises his finger and looks expectantly to one side, and everyone else quietly looks with him. Then the man shakes his head: no, it wasn't anything. The guests begin to move again, they laugh mindlessly, making fun of the man who had reminded them to listen, and had just transformed a crowd of strangers into one focused flock of listeners, if only for a few seconds.

. . .

In a restaurant, a rather large group of young men and women has gotten up to leave. The check has been paid, and they're all heading for the door engaged in lively discourse. But there is one woman still sitting at her table contemplating the horrible thing one of them just said. The others are already standing in the foyer when her husband turns around and goes back to the table. As he was about to go out the door, he had noticed that his wife was missing. But she was already standing up when he approached, and walked right past him on out through both doors.

. . .

In their home, at the stroke of an indeterminate hour, after many years of being dazed, exhausted, and trying to separate, two people are looking at each other through wide open eyes. A sense of recognition draws them together, a kind of desire, as if in the end only the arousal of all sexual powers, like a revolution, could free them from the burden of their mutual story and bring it to an end. A longing for closure flows out of every street they ever walked down together, arm in arm. A longing that they both are sensing as pure revolt. They embrace each other with clenched arms in which their intimacy, their memory, their hopelessly long companionship – in which the entire matter of their mutual awareness is entwined, rushing into naked blackness like a dying star.

. . .

Despite and in the midst of a bout of determined ill will, which arose after a quarrel between them, and as a result of which they spent two days of their trip under the pressure of extreme silence, the woman, still picking disinterestedly at her filet, suddenly raises her head and amorously hums along with an old hit blaring out of the speakers at the bar. The man looks at her as if she has not only taken leave of her senses, but has lost every last trace of rationality.

Every love is based on its own utopia. And this miserable partnership has its sources in the grayness of a primeval time surfeited with good fortune and song. Its beginning is preserved as a moment frozen solid in the heart of the woman. There is still *illud tempus* in her, where over the course of time everything has decayed terribly and changed. Initial point, frozen, solid, not very nutritious provisions for the journey.

. . .

During their first hour, two people still toying with the beginning are now so late, each returning to a family, to a spouse, that they must dash through this unfamiliar quarter of the city to catch a subway train that will carry them home with a delay hardly to be perceived. The haste, the wind, the stumbling dash shake free the confession that would not yet have come out during quieter moments. And while they are running, the woman two steps ahead of the man, he gasps it out after her. With his screams, like a jockey's encouragements low on the neck of a race horse, he pushes his lover forward faster and faster, as if happiness were giving her the whip. In the rush, she can hardly turn her head to yell back into the air that she loves him, too. Then they are both lost in the crowds and don't see each other until the next day.

. . .

I will hear it for a long time: the cries of the woman who was about to leap from the top floor of an apartment hotel one morning. At first it was a dull, steady cry that only slowly emerged out of the dense noises of the street. The hotel was immediately adjacent to the building where I was staying, so I was unable to see the incipient leaper herself, but I could see the circle of expectation that had formed across the street from her lonely station. At the roofline, the building is about fifteen, at the most, twenty meters high; it seems doubtful that a jump into such shallow depths would necessarily end in death, but rather in horrible injury. Her screams grew louder, now she was yelling in a very high, plaintive and almost jubilant voice: "Help! . . . Help!" A queen of most dire straits, little by little she collected a small nation at her feet, the vassals of her rule of pain. Everywhere in the many windows of the office buildings across the street, diagonally opposite the hotel, employees leaped up from their desks, pushing and shoving, and turning their eyes to the heights. But the hesitant sovereign of the windowsill had not long kept her subjects in breathless awe before the police and the fire department arrived. At the approach of the sirens – and here this word again alternated back and forth between its old meaning, the song of seduction rising out of the depths, and its current one, of the lifesaver's alarm – the woman yelled louder and louder, more and more plaintively: "Help . . . help," and "Now listen to me!" But she had absolutely nothing else to say other than once again: Help, help. The firemen unrolled their jumping tarp and six of them together held it stretched out under the window. But they were hardly casting a serious look skyward, they were much more interested in the staring faces of the crowd, and were happy for every gaze directed toward their skilled grip and powerfully braced bodies. They were doing their duty, and they looked around the circle at each other. They knew she wouldn't jump. After they had cast only a fleeting but experienced eye over the posture, position, and gestures of the candidate, these men apparently knew the fall would not be here. And right, a little later she, a young woman with bright blonde bangs over her forehead, accompanied by the police and strapped down to a stretcher, was carried out of the hotel and loaded into an ambulance. Saved.

She was seen again that evening. On the regional television news broadcast, we are introduced to people who had recently survived a suicide attempt. We are present as people who had overdosed on sleeping pills awake, and we are there every second of the way as they open their eyes to a new existence right into the television camera.

The impression one gets of the rescued persons is generally disappointing. Belatedly, they find nothing to say, or only the dullest expression to describe their situation before the great transformation. Also remarkable, how little they question their surroundings: they seem to grasp immediately that they have come to in a clinic bed, and not in the realm of the dead. The first thing a few of them do is go to the sink and brush their teeth. The young woman who was intending to jump out of the hotel window tells the TV news team: "Peter's so damned jealous. I couldn't tell where I was anymore. I just didn't have any choice." Once described this way, and the scream of the one so elevated this morning, her determination to follow through on this final, most lofty of human acts seems to be canceled out by this human, all too comprehensible, and thus trivial motive. Still, the real misery is, that the real misery cannot find expression. It degrades one's consciousness, it cannot break out. Great agony inhabits a thousand trivial agonies. As long as she keeps babbling, and doesn't fall, she will continue to play this two-handed game with Peter and death . . .

. . .

Recently, one evening, after a particularly harrowing day, Ulf's lover went home to her husband in the early hours of the day and found her apartment half burned out. Her husband had tried to put out the fire, the fire department had come and every room was now under water. It would have taken very little for the flames to have spread to the children's rooms.

She often seemed vacant and indifferent, but was, this particular evening, remarkably alert and unusually involved in our conversation without ever saying a word. We were once more discussing the question of how art might play a more positive role in our lives. Art, after all, could not help being bound up with a life-enhancing, life-sustaining agenda. Indeed, it must make a primary contribution to providing the era of reflection with new content. A new art, Ulf added, would, first and foremost, have to liberate itself from the simply paradoxical, simply critical, simply the intelligence exposing what is false, through whose vacuous forms what had already been thought through was trickling away into dilution. Instead of this, it would have to take up the great, portentous Yes (of a Rilke, for example). The constructive, the challenging forces, the creative, and the endowing in its entirety, not the critical, are to be the realm of our future aesthetic aspirations. Song – Pound, and Rilke over and over again – must never be allowed to grow silent!

His lover quietly spoke along with everything that was being said. Not that she raised any objections, had anything to add or to question, no, she simply mumbled to herself, it was only the vibration of her vocal cords producing the sound of speech. It was not unlike some mentally ill who involuntarily echo the sounds they hear when someone speaks to them. Nonetheless, she was agitated and had something to say to everything. But the volume and the articulation of her observations were weak, below the threshold of distinct expression. For example, I happened to use the word "sensuality" and immediately retracted it. But she had already snapped it up and said, without being particularly coherent: "Sensuality, basically a good word, the senses!" and as she was speaking, she grabbed Ulf by the arm in order to demonstrate the fundamentally simple and manifest meaning of the word. But not even that was to be a viable contribution to our discussion, we hardly paid any attention to her, and she knew it, or she would have kept silent the way she always had. But somehow, that evening she had to speak, speak along with the rest of us, no matter how, and this urge seemed stronger than the pain and embarrassment of always being ignored.

. . .

From time to time, when she feels like it, she goes out looking for a strong, well-dressed guy, and most of the time she finds what she's looking for. It doesn't cost her anything. They are body friends. They know very little about each other, nothing more than can be communicated during a cigarette break and then forgotten. This is the way it is done, exactly as described, even recommended, in a thousand magazines. The role model of two people helping each other to live the single and uncommitted life they prefer. In front of the house, she takes leave of the man in the white trousers, caressing him across one cheek. Tender and thankful is how it appears, knowing and not indecent. A complete gesture of both the vapid kindness as well as the abundance of possible exits which have come to characterize loving independent of love. What we are really dealing with here is a liberal democratic institution, free of chaos and anxiety, love subordinated to the good, domesticated and dedicated to freedom. Anxiety belongs to atomic power plants. No one is any longer required to endure it at its sexual source. And many even seem to have succeeded in provincializing anxiety, transferring it to another site.

Even hearing the word *affairs*, again and again, is enough to turn sweaty palms dry. As vacuous as it may sound, it is an attempt at artificially sobering and casting a spell of accountability over a sphere which is still the most primal, impenetrable, and consuming passion in us. It may be that total permissiveness, continual consumption will change something, loosening and weakening all ties. The way someone without a past takes pleasure in the cold staging of history, the abrupt tableaus of Prussians, Staufers, and the tombs of the pharaohs, and this is how it will come to be that almost nothing else but the forensic evidence of love will excite the loveless. They would dearly love to experience what a so-called erotic adventure really was, or to know the kind of passion that could not flourish until it had first broken through rules, customs, and resistance.

For those of us in the cities, mobile, hurried and heterogenous, the choice of partners takes place in the "free" play of attracting and repelling forces, according to our whims and desires and the available stimuli. It is as if erotic reality, the external scene of varying opportunity, had become a perfect representation of the soul, with its bewildering, chaotic desires and abundance of ambivalences. We will never again meet the person whom we know, from the very first, suits us like no other, the only right one for us. Given our current lifestyle, in which we are becoming more and more independent of one another while at the same time becoming more and more dependent on the whole, such a sleight of heart is no longer of any use, and we will gradually drop it from our repertoire of feeling. Now, when the soul hardly needs to obey external demands, the unbridled dominion of internal ambivalences makes itself felt ever more strongly. Any reference to bonds that rest solely on feeling and are no longer required to fulfill any common social destiny becomes a complex Yes-No, and its indivisible core is Love-Cold. All that matters is what is currently pleasing to the soul – and, as we all know, currently, nothing is pleasing, for the soul is the refuge, per se, of immediacy. Any encounter which takes place in an environment of this extreme external freedom and irresponsibility will soon become a ruined victim of obsession, the desires, and destructive drives, of the subconscious. In this realm – where the demands of society (building a community, reproduction, maintaining tradition, etc.) are no longer a dominant force, impulse consorts unconstrained with opportunity, superficial attraction and the novel with the swift change of address – out of this broad flow of traffic, where what is desired can be so quickly had, no bond can possibly emerge, no matter how truly pledged. This current flows through all of us.

. . .

Visit from M. Four years after our divorce she is returning a book, and now, in new clothes and shorter hair, is again sitting on the same window seat she was sitting on our last night together. She's very relaxed and immediately begins speaking about "us." That back then, I had all but expunged everything positive in her. That I had never had anything but contempt for her career, her mother, her tastes, her background. Not one loving word, but every mean thing I ever said seems to be fresh in her memory, and she is quoting me word for word. Hardly amusing! And encounters like this are supposed to recast the pain of the past into today's flirtation, the flirtation of experience. So empty and tedious to be saying those things coolly and calmly, which back then would have been blurted out in enough panic to turn us both pale. Could she possibly have been thinking of me all this time in terms of this lifeless conjecture? If we weren't already divorced, it seems to me this would truly be grounds: that she is not capable of remembering us in pain and generosity. I winced when she suddenly gave me a good-bye kiss. Not ever again! Not ever you again!

. . .

She had inherited a house, the petite young woman, employee of the municipal transportation office, she is speaking enthusiastically about the house of her grandmother, recently deceased, nothing but nooks!, trying to entice a male colleague who is already married but stays the weekend. Plans, plans. She makes a sketch of the house for him on a paper napkin, hoping to lure him there. At this drastic change in her life, she can hardly contain herself, she raves and unnerves herself and ever more insistently tries to persuade a silent stranger to share his future with her. For his part, the man begins nervously twisting his wedding band around his finger, smiles incredulously, gently shakes his head as if this were all too amazing, and then silently tries these changes out on himself, from the calves on up.

. . .

A municipal worker in his mid-thirties lets the engines of his intelligence hum for the benefit of the mute and inert wife sitting next to him. He aims the light of his critique at certain incidents in the office, he elevates himself to the status of disinterested observer of his own department, now, in the evening, while enjoying an after-work drink at the bar. As she can neither be expected to protest nor see through his foolishness, he keeps talking louder and louder, more and more grandly, about the abuses in the administration and what he intends to do about them. And since he is just talking to himself and does not have to take anyone else into consideration, he keeps feeling his intelligence soar, and his insight into the inner workings of things is intoxicating. Then, all of a sudden, he sees admiration in his wife's eyes; for his own sense of accomplishment he needs her to be somewhat brighter than she is, and that's how he imagines her to be. The way she is sitting next to him, so unthreatening and dependent, this person is the best possible narcotic he could have to make himself feel important. Despite the fact that she now and again, letting fall an inappropriate interjection, betrays how truly uninterested she is, how she is just not on the "same wavelength" – a shortcoming in their partnership which has many a time caused the young office worker to seek his pleasures elsewhere, and then bitterly regret. He (well into his diatribe against the department): "Do you have any idea what that's costing the taxpayer!" She: "Isn't there any other department that could take care of it?" He: "Hardly! Just imagine what it's costing the taxpayer!" And repeats what he said with great emphasis, almost irate, in order to get his wife as wound up as he is. But it's just not in her nature, there isn't anyone or anything that can make her really indignant. Then, suddenly, he stops talking and no further question, no more exacting inquiry is forthcoming from her side. The man pays the waiter and a little while later they both get up. As he is holding her coat for her to slip into, and they are looking at each other, there is the involuntary and indelible glimmer of a tender compassion in his eyes.

. . .

In a tavern with a very mixed clientele, we discover a man in his early forties, a person who to judge by his appearance is particularly tractable, and for his generation rather timid, an office worker in a dead-end job, who wants to look around a little on Saturday night, and next to him there is a rather plump little woman with a mouth like a duck's bill. They are both perched nervously, or (as they would like to believe) are casually seated, at the bar, where they are tightly encircled by gays, dealers, transvestites, and drag queens. Every Saturday they make an excursion into the scene and sense, not entirely without inner exhilaration, how everything which represents the middle, the majority, the average is suddenly, here in this other milieu, characteristic of the outsider. Their journey, from an outer precinct of the city into the center, is actually one from the middle to the periphery: the philistines have become the exotics. Even though the air in the tavern is hot and stuffy, the wife keeps her fur hat on her head, it's winter outside. Sitting down on the vacant barstools next to them is a gay couple with their little bags, their eau sauvage, their silk shirts. Here, the harmless man and his wife look at each other – this is something they would call "meaningful" – and they are forced to repress a giggle. Something strangely left behind, undeveloped, something teenagelike emanates from them, from both of them, no difference at all. Still, they are good together, they're not concealing anything unfriendly, nothing aggressive about their faces. On the one hand, as chaste as a couple of Red Chinese lovers, they have also become addicted to this completely perverse voyeurism, which they can no longer do without and in search of which they are drawn again and again to these sites of tired, long since disenchanted depravity. Looking at this peculiar couple, one wonders which realm of sexual exile they inhabit in this wretched, collective fucking and ex-society. One imagines their embraces always ending the same way: the little wife raises her eyebrows inquiringly and smiles a gentle though not entirely unconstrained smile, while her husband opens his quivering lids, and neither of them has noticed when it actually happened. But then they hold each other close. She is the one who is becoming more and more insistent on driving into the city in order to feel the vibrations of these meeting places, with their crazy mixed-up classes, their stimuli entirely distinct from the offerings of the cheap pleasure palaces, where the meagerness of simple exposure leaves nothing more to imagine, to espy, to discover. The woman from the bedroom suburbs is on her way to becoming a determined dreamer without having to leave her husband, but still leading rather than following him in this transformation. Both of them have always been ready to chortle *together* about the imperfection of love.

. . .

Her realm is obscenity. The young laboratory technician lives in a summer night's dream of sexual echoes and metamorphoses. Wherever she sits, wherever she looks, everything is full of sexual allusion and she has to say *it*, incessantly, even if it is a minute observation about a cigarette in an ashtray, about the language that insinuates itself into another's ear. At a restaurant for

Sunday dinner with the family – father, mother on one side of the table, she alone on the other – she immediately sets out to do only one thing: to turn her parents on, to spread an atmosphere of new German, bourgeois innuendo all across their midday repast. She refers to herself as the hottest item in the entire X-ray lab, and relates in detail how her boss recently sat down next to her in the sauna, where everyone is the same, but then again not really all the same. She is talking to her parents as if they were casual acquaintances made at a Club Med; even with them, or perhaps especially with them, the only language she has is the language of the suggestive. Still, she seeks neither to provoke others nor to liberate herself, but rather to establish a common temper, consonance, a shared ringing laughter. It is rather remarkable that the mother quickly picks up on the vibrations emanating from her child, giggling at first, but then becoming more and more intimate, more crude, making no attempt to withhold the undisguised allusions which keep honing in on the masculinity of the father. The daughter is describing her father as a "physical specimen" with enormously broad shoulders, narrow pelvis and – shared laughter of both women. But the physical specimen is sitting comfortably silent at the table, a solid citizen who likes to chuckle but is still a little embarrassed. Together, the two women let their fantasies go, praising his charms in highly suggestive tones, while the upright and silent figure of the father leaves no doubt that his position in the family has always rested on money and goodness, and not on the virtuosity of his lovemaking. The mother, with her high bent nose, blinks at the daughter and brazenly takes on her offspring's air: these days she sometimes leaves her nightgown hanging in the bathroom. Shrill laughter from the daughter: "Look, Daddy's ears are turning red!" And soon after that, the elf from the tanning salon stretches out in her long white men's shirt, and says to her father: "I don't know how you are in bed, I haven't got the slightest idea now that you've put down your knife and your fork . . ." And so on. We are undecided: is this a particularly coarse creature or is she really haunted by pornocratic darkness? It is certain that every one of her attempts to communicate with her fellow human beings must be this lively – and for her, what is lively is obscene. She is demanding, poor, lonely, knows as much or as little about depravity as everyone else. But she speaks. She expresses *it*. And so doing, she acts out a form of eroticism, not so much a form of sex. She speaks, she demands *it* – what? Actually nothing more than the unstoppable, endlessly flooding torrent of her own obscene speech, and the pleasure of immersing herself in the river of this speech. Her fantasy is not especially fertile, what she sees and remarks is not grotesque, still sometimes she is inventive, we know she is not well read and it suddenly seems as if a language has sprouted up right over her head. But often enough she is unable to grasp anything out of the air, which is filled with an overabundance of sexual spirits, and then her darkness turns boutique, and she begins making use of the flat-footed clichés from television's treasure chest. At this point, her summer night's dream has no more wondrous magic than her lab boss transformed into a naked body at the sauna.

• • •

The life of a mother-to-be, in a circle of mothers-to-be, everyone building a solid front, roughly in accord; pregnancy club meets at Helen's every Tuesday, the only interloper a grumpy old janitor. Enlightened, pale, having just given up smoking, rather greasy hair, jeans and T-shirt topped off with a folk-art sweater, thirsting for even more enlightenment ("literature" they call it, terse and comprehensive), wanting most of all a permanent discussion in order to protect themselves from good fortune, bad fortune, and everything else unfathomable. Helen's husband, lawyer, blond, distinctly balding, beard, joined the Social Democratic Party in the fourth month of her pregnancy. His taste for Scandinavian knockdown furniture dominates the look of their three-and-a-half room apartment. Solid, modern, two-party relationship. They are relaxed and affectionate with each other, without the least exaggeration, without a flame. The "so-called irrational" has been tackled and brought under control by the use of just this cliché. Their attitude toward career and duty is, as much as possible, decidedly one of pleasure. Lots of things are fun. While making love they made a child. She is carrying her baby in this open nook full of togetherness, and the mothers-to-be in her neighborhood share their experiences and worries, now somewhat anxiously, as they will soon deliver and know almost nothing of the most natural things. So many warm united nestmakers, given the least consensus within which people protect their own little microcosms, in order to have something with which to confront the terrible macrocosm of the world outside. And this is the way it should be. For a single person, there is nothing anywhere around but the abyss (even for the aggressively self-deluded individual who believes it is not so). We are left with nothing to do but shoulder our part of even the craziest social junk: Father, mother, daughter found a Parent-Child Group and provide themselves with a safety net of children's kits and self-help advisory councils, with workshops for everything, plenary sessions at the local bar, and the psychotherapy of the mobile urban zone. But still: how we yearn to be able to distinguish ourselves from these people of the hour, totally and entirely of today. How unsatisfying it would be if we were nothing but today's model. Passion, life itself, needs access to the past (even more than anticipation), it gathers its energies from realms that no longer exist, from historical memory. But where do we find . . . ? Belonging in the shallow pocket of the safety net has replaced being cut off at the roots; the diachronic, the vertical construct is suspended in air.

. . .

A curious young woman came in, accompanied by, but not having any relationship to, a man who brought me some news, and soon left without her.

She stayed sitting in my chair without either invitation or explanation, and when I looked at her silently, she laughed, a quiet, mysterious laugh which hardly veiled her intentions. I had never met her before, I hadn't even caught her name. Now she was firmly ensconced in my bookstall and her true appearance became entangled in a web of countless ideals, secret expectations, reserved pleasures. The prey, turning itself over, surprises the idle hunter, even mocks him. At first, we begin to digest this kind of catch, this kind of alien body with a lot of talk. The mouth overflows when the eyes cannot believe what they are seeing. But the young woman is not pretending her way into the mysterious, what she is really doing is unburdening herself of a lot of rambling chatter about art and current events. In a first hour of this kind, matters of opinion begin to pile up. At the same time, we are cautiously looking for the hidden catch in this free offer. There must be something wrong with her or she wouldn't just be here. In any case, her voice is conspicuous, the way it sounds so unsteady, the way her sure pitch sometimes just slips away, the occurrence of unusually strong variation in volume. Like a deaf person who cannot really control her own voice, she unexpectedly speaks too loudly and intensely given the modest content of her message and the proximity of the listener. I learn that she is a twin. But must be, it seems to me: a twin of her mother. At this point, her words suddenly become firm and smart, her hands are no longer fidgeting, they're wiping the table, they flap around in the air like the hands of a nagging housewife in the stairwell. Her entire camouflage, her psycho-armor is exposed, it is her mother, and when we open the visor and look down into the navel we find the little one looking back up in trepidation. And in this way, many of us are weak who have entered *freely*, forced to be free, one might say, because these days no one escapes the outward freedom of lifestyles. At the age of fifteen, the first steady relationship, still it lasted five years with all the dictates of a marriage; at twenty, again utterly alone: she pulls the cap of house and hearth down over her ears whenever she senses peril around her, and there is a mother's voice croaking out from under it. Our touches grow into a grotesque act of separation. I sensed it dully, but I cannot extricate myself so quickly from the stormy fantasies of my freshly aroused amorousness. I should have known from her open, empty, totally yielding mouth that with my torrent of words every bit of energy needed to respond had dried up. For my part, I held to my words, I enticed her body, adored it with tender utterance, for without them I would never have been able to hold or endure this stranger at all. But she, in the middle of an embrace, suddenly says: "I'm starting to be afraid of you!" Because I seem too ardent to her. I hardly hear what she's saying and could not do anything, anyway, to stop teaching her fear with my caresses. For her, my words brought an aspect of utter nonsense into the act, which would never have happened if I had taken her dumbly and had not myself sought some refuge with her. We make our exchanges, we discuss, and once we are exhausted we sleep – but silently – together, quiet! After all, it is really nothing more than the continuation of a nascent sympathy by other means. Strange: the same way I had reacted to the extremes in her voice, she was later shocked at the transformations in my language from table to bed, from opinion to memory, from asserting to whispering, from knowing to stammering.

. . .

In Blönduós on the north coast of Iceland, and in the Blönduós Hotel, which has no restaurant. The only place I can get something to eat is at the Esso gas station: a chalky-white chicken leg in Gallert. A street lamp, gray and small, like a shop light in a garage, shines in front of a one-story house with a tongue-red roof. The sea is shifting from brown to green, depending on the cloud cover and the depth of the water. Above the shore, dusty green grass-covered hills where lambs grazed. Four lonesome telegraph poles are standing there as if only keeping in contact among themselves. A closed and empty loop, torn out of the worldwide network like this ungainly little place itself, secretly yearning for even greater remoteness, toward a more distant, devouring North. And always this light of an artificially postponed earliness, uncertain whether it is an early evening or an early morning, even at midnight on a lava black beach under a cloudy lava black sky, when the sun breaks through, and quickly, like glory's searchlight, sweeps across the barren land.

Here, after the evil deed is done, after larceny, after a serious crime committed against humanity? Looking out to sea always means waiting for something; some kind of arrival is always being intimated, ship or flotsam, cadaver, nymph or sea monster – the sea will bring it into being. It is the element that cannot listen at all. It alone is the speaking, without judgment and accord; disobedient, without an ear for earth. It is the entirety of a melody without contradiction. The earth lies in a hollow gesture, like the curvature of a question turned toward the water. The question mark has the outline of an ear. The ear only receives, like the womb. All forms are sexual, pointed and round, until they vanish in spirit; and the masculine answer penetrates the womb question.

. . .

Akureyri, the port city, lies one hundred and fifty kilometers to the east, an old woman standing at the reception desk of the Edda Hotel. It is a school building which is converted into a tourist hostel during the summer. In every single hallway, the smell of milk soup. In very careful German, the woman asks the girl behind the desk how long she, she and her husband, who has quietly gone upstairs with both suitcases, may stay in their room the next morning . . . The girl answers awkwardly, scratches the words out of her throat: "Eh . . . until half past eleven." Then the old woman, solicitous and careful, continues to speak about the arrangements for their departure the next morning. How late can they get breakfast, how can they get a taxi? The girl at the reception croaks: "First street to the left, second to the right." The old woman says: "We feel so fortunate to have gotten this room." Now, instead of becoming more simple, her speech becomes more articulate, for the sake of clarity. She folds her hands on the desk and continues to speak slowly, rather excessively pleased but without any trace of hypocrisy, and we might say that she has truly put her heart into this superfluous conversation. Fortunate, she and her husband are, it is after all high season and they had not made reservations – "High Season?" she asks again, uncertain whether she has been understood or not. Then, once more she thanks the young Icelandic woman effusively, just as if this woman had, out of great personal generosity, done her utmost to make them welcome.

The next morning, the old woman and her husband, who had not been seen that evening, having immediately gone upstairs after their arrival, are found lying next to one another dead, narrow beds pushed together in their much praised room. They had both taken poison and lay as they had wanted, hand in hand, on their backs. They had managed to withstand the brief, severe cramps in their intertwined, almost breaking fingers. In the end, it turned out that the woman was suffering from a terminal illness, and this is what had driven them to take a step they would never have dared take at home, where they were living under one roof with daughter, son-in-law, and grandchildren. So, they die away from home at the end of a trip to Iceland, leaving behind their well-ordered papers, money, and a very precise itinerary for "After Leaving Life." The old man, her loyal follower, had not spoken for a very long time. Once the arrangements had been made, he seemed to find it necessary not to add a single word, and immediately enter into silence.

. . .

A married couple, alcoholics, is standing in line at the cash register in the *Quelle* department store. Mumbling and staring at the floor, the man keeps to his wife's side. Without external cause, she pinches her right eye shut several times, as if she were sharing a lustful secret with some invisible being. Her damaged nerves replay a short program over and over again. At brief intervals, provoked by a reflexive shock, she abruptly jerks her head around and smiles a smile, as friendly as it is distorted in fear, in a direction where no one is standing, and from where no one calls. An erratic drama is being played out over her reddened, puffy, wrinkled face, precipitated solely by the crush of standing in line, crowded together with so many strangers. In all directions, the smile, the shards of a smile, seem to amicably fend off too much crowding. The mouth with its bright, shiny grimace exposes a stubby row of teeth, from left to right growing stubbier and stubbier, with more and more cavities. She is purchasing a lemon yellow alarm clock. Why set an alarm? So she can get up for her first swig? I was standing at the main entrance next to a glass door, waiting with an unwieldy piece of garden furniture for my friend, who was bringing the rest of the pieces. The alcoholic couple came out just as we were loading our freight for the journey home. And the woman remarked to her husband that it was particularly clever of us to be fumbling around with our bulky purchases right at the exit. Although we weren't really in their way, she seemed quite pleased to find herself in the right and us a nuisance, and to be able to remark on the situation. My friend growled at her rudely: "Shut up, you old cow." When I heard this, I felt as if I had seen someone step on the stomach of an accident victim. I had been observing their fate for some time and felt nothing but sympathy for them. When we passed them both on the street, the woman stopped her husband and said quietly, as if someone famous were going by: "Did he really call me an old cow!" "Who?" the man asked. "That guy," the woman said, nodding in our direction. She had tried with so much prophylactic smiling and spectral accommodation to ward off anything around her which could possibly do her harm, still, in the end, it had hurt. Truly distressed, and not in anger, she stopped and repeated the insult, and it seemed even more outrageous.

. . .

In a film about an Indian tribe in the Amazon jungle, we see a mother sitting naked in front of her small child who is screaming from terrible stomach cramps. The mother is talking to the sick boy, but there is nothing she can do, she does not know how to help him. All at once we can feel what a terrible prison, what an agony of helplessness it is not to know what we know, we over-civilized, about saving a life in an emergency. This predicament seems all the more distressing and utterly nightmarish because the gestures of sorrow, fear, pain are exactly the same as ours, and we do not really want to admit that internally this intimate mode of expression might be governed by an entirely different sense of being. A precisely delimited consciousness, which views its world with alert, masterful eyes, free of yearning and wonder, suspicion and doubt; an intelligence for the hunt, for belief, and the living community, knowing neither greed nor selfishness. And sitting in the grass not knowing what to do, this woman lays hands, warmed by the fire, on the child's stomach and rubs warm animal blood over it. Only warmth, this is all the medicine she has to give. But the boy dies. We can already see his backside turning reddish blue. His mother puts a black sweater on him, perhaps the most valuable object she has ever owned. Her tribe knows how to throw pots and trades their vessels with neighboring tribes for a variety of the junk civilization has to offer. She is putting the sweater on a corpse. She begs the child to say something, to open his eyes, to start screaming again. And she cries for a long time, pressing her eyes shut again and again, as if she were squeezing out the tears.

A short time later the dead boy is buried in a very shallow grave out at the edge of the village. The mother leaves the sweater on the body and lays a bottle of water and a cup into the grave for the long journey. Once the grave has been covered over and all the other women, who had stood by her at the burial but not during her son's death throes, have left, she sits before the closed earth, struck by the loss of her child, and once more calls plaintively for him to return. But by the next morning, the grief seems to have passed. She joins the others on an expedition to one of the neighboring tribes with whom they trade, the march will mean seven hours of slogging over the muddy, rain-soaked floor of the jungle. The dead child, once sent off on his journey, now belongs to a sphere which the living must not touch and where no grief-filled memory may follow. The rite provides release with an abrupt forgetting as fresh as the dew.

And don't we grieve so long and so dolefully mainly because we are profoundly alone in any case, and our social bonds never really go beyond the two-person unit in which we isolate ourselves with that one other person: mother, father, lover, child? With the loss of *one* beloved being our whole world crumbles, showing us what a nonsocial existence we lead. There is no living community for which our forgetting and our energy is absolutely crucial to its self-preservation, and the self-preservation of each of its members.

. . .

An American soldier, who deserted in 1949, had been in hiding for almost thirty years in West Berlin. He found refuge in the apartment of his German girlfriend, who took care of him and shielded him from the outside world. Until she died. He got his only impressions of a precipitously evolving reality from television and from what his girlfriend told him. He had not even once dared go out on the balcony. He was so unfamiliar with the everyday details of his environment that after emerging from his isolation to call the police and finally turn himself in as a deserter, he was unable to use a German coin phone. He simply didn't know how to do it. He had to ask a passerby to show him.

. . .

A professionally frustrated man, his wife, and a door which will not close. "Can't you finally fix the damned door!" the wife yells. The man's discouraged but carpenterly grip on the door, his boundless melancholy at having to *fiddle around* with the door.

. . .

He hunches down on the floor with his knees pressed into his chest, gently rocking on his cheeks. Selecting out of an abundance of life's offerings, his wife bends over him with an outstretched arm: "And what about some sun?" The man shrugs his shoulders indifferently and keeps rocking, unmoved. No desire.

"The world is full of happening and may even already be in a state of radical upheaval. And all you can do is sit there rocking back and forth."

. . .

A man and a woman, both translators of American English, are living in almost monkish isolation among the poorly soundproofed walls of a small, new apartment stuffed full of thousands of books, countless stacks of magazines, they are both magazine freaks, and on top of that they both sit themselves down in front of the radio several times a day in order to keep up with what's going on in politics and intellectual life, world news, even reports from distant battlefields, over shortwave, and this all takes place according to a precise daily schedule and a program plan which they put together once each week.

In this lair full of current events, in which two so infinitely apprised heads, one might even say over-informed, so polished they gleam, cannot possibly avoid one another, there are no longer debates and argumentation of the kind usually found among committed and involved people. What the two of them are really presenting is a duel of world views, or better put: they spin around in a swift dance of political positions, which they alternately take up against one another. If *he* feels like defending the most recent foreign policy guidelines of the Communist party, then *she* will quote to him from the Charter of Unaligned Nations, or rebut his stance in the spirit of the Islamic Liberation Movement. If, on the other hand, it comes to questions of West German immigration policy, and he takes a liberal, pro-immigrant stance, then she will promptly sideswipe him with a couple of sharp-tongued retorts:

"The child of whose soul is our nation to become? What can the teachers possibly teach in a class where twenty percent of the pupils are immigrants?" If, on another occasion, he dares to bring up the Italian Fascist remnants of the anarcho-syndicalists, he will be countered by a fierce lecture delivered from the standpoint of Proletarian Internationalism. If, in a tormented half hour, she paints a picture of a solar-atomic state of the future, a mega-industrial power rising up out of extreme crises and trials, and possessing a level of ruthlessness never before known, against this he carefully holds up outlines of a gentle revolution, sketches of a postindustrial service society where the majority of people are engaged in life-enhancing and leisure services industries. These are the kinds of exchanges they share day in and day out, shifting their positions from left to right, then and now, between optimism and pessimism, and not infrequently one person's argument today reappears tomorrow as the other's counterargument. In their dialogues, all political fundament dissolves into a plethora of scenarios and conflict-resolution models, providing inexhaustible opportunity for play and mutual stimulation. One could even think of it as *l'art pour l'art* of pure opposition, if ardor were not at the core, inspiring them both – a smart, unfulfilled love, as strong as it was on the first day, maintaining itself and flourishing behind closed curtains, in a continuously refreshing stream of data, in the warm refuge of worldviews.

. . .

The two old sisters sit next to one another at the telephone. The husband of one sister was again taken to the hospital. Incurably tired of life, no sleep will bring him back. The hard, pulsing ring of the telephone, and behind it the so quiet and miserable voice of the old man lying on his sickbed. One last long-distance conversation. Disembodied, the connection now hanging on nothing but one sense, the sense of hearing. The very next conversation will be a memory. So, withdrawing little by little from the external senses of the sisters, he passes into their minds' sense.

. . .

Singing along, the lips of a dancing woman who is leaning back into the stylish, sophisticated lead of her husband. They are dancing to a hit of the False Fifties, Tuesday evenings in the *Resi*, the old Berlin pleasure palace, which in the meantime has been hit by the steel wrecker's ball, so now much of it is ground level. The man can hardly remember the words but growls along here and there during the refrain, while doing the slow foxtrot the woman in his arms silently lip-synchs the whole song, like a whisper in a dream, she still knows every line by heart. But who is she turning to in this melody of her memory? Involuntarily her head sways, and, pale at the reunion, she gazes out of this couple into the corners of the cold hall revolving around her. There is no shared remembering.

. . .

Tuesdays in the *Resi*. How sad, such a cool empty ballroom that belongs only to the masses, and can only be heated by the flurry of their exertions. They don't come here any more. Coming out of the pneumatic mail tube at the table of a lonely guest from the retirement home, there was a draft, a veritable blast of air, and he thought to himself: this can't be the darkness from below trying to suck you in, stealthily. At this point, a container shot out of the tube and he opened it with trembling fingers, and there was a note inside. But it was something in Norwegian or Swedish, table 261, that was where he was being invited to introduce himself, or call using the telephone on the table. But Scandinavian? Doesn't understand it at all. A group of tourists, ladies and gentlemen from Scandinavia who wish to let themselves be charmed once more by the *Resi*, our beautiful old pleasure palace. And they're sending him a note, but he doesn't understand it and he stays sitting right where he is. But it pleased him.

The pneumatic postal service has enabled another gentleman from the retirement residence at the Zoological Garden to win himself a place at the table of two elderly ladies, two friends from Brix, somewhat elegant, made up somewhat too eager to look younger, with soft, high-heeled boots on their skinny legs. They already know what they've reeled in: Another funny man! Still, he's better than the mute old stiffneck they had picked up in the Kempinski, or the incessant whiner from Potsdam.

This one could at least make you laugh, one of those good-natured German sorts you find in every group, young or old, in almost every office, in your extended family, on every group trip, even in every school class. Until now, this kind of character has only been readily found among males, and if there were ever to be one last, completely depraved preserve of masculinity and masculine conquest behavior, then it would probably be our sad fate to see it populated by the manic funny man. Although no one finds him genuinely attractive as a person, he always has a more significant influence on his milieu than we might assume, given his stale jokes and the laughter they provoke. In a smaller group, we are never really certain either about his motives or his status. At first, he seems to be nothing more than the most banal sort of outsider: one everyone else agrees with. One driven toward the middle, who out of a particularly severe sense of isolation feels the need to position himself at the center, one who must make up for his abnormal lack of amicable relationships with a wild excess of dumb stuff that appeals to the crowd and is immediately pleasing. As long as he keeps everyone laughing, no one will ask what's wrong with this joker, what about him might be infirm. Still, his ceaseless bantering is no less a madness than someone else's crazy screaming or stammer. But: since it is frolicking around the hackneyed and the commonplace, it can survive in any order-loving society, because laughter is always healthy. However, viewing this man from some distance and with some objectivity, we can clearly see the traits of a frustrated, profoundly undirected obsessiveness. Then, all of a sudden, he looks to us like a failed artist totally consumed by his own mediocrity. In his sycophantic way, this lonely stand-up comedian keeps performing a crude parody of our own loneliness. We can immediately see a hopeless compulsion to joke, and feel, sometimes almost frighteningly, how terribly alone he is. For his audience, there is really neither anything desirable nor repulsive about the role in which he is forcing himself on them. They are no more interested in standing in his shoes than they are in wrapping them around his ears. There is no one who hasn't secretly seen him for the poor wretch he is, and yet he has undertaken a very significant task for them all. For example, in a group that is just beginning to form, he is most often the character who first becomes distinct; there is nothing else he can do: he has to call attention to himself. But he is very seldom the one whom the others subsequently follow. All he can do with his jokes is prepare the others to listen to the one who will eventually lead. He is basically the jester who makes his appearance in order to introduce the king. When a suitable leader then steps forth, he distances himself from the joker, who does nothing but hawk tired old sayings, put everyone in a good mood, and who has absolutely nothing to offer should he ever be called upon to confront a serious challenge.

Now, this aging clown in the *Resi* is basically the type who likes to hear himself talk, a humorist and a braggart, too, who does not hesitate to wave his own flag: certainly no one would find it boring to relive the old days with him. As if playing down from a vaudeville stage, he entertains the two ladies, telling them that in spite of being retired he still travels to West Germany now and then, as a salesman, and what adventures hasn't he had. Not long ago in Frankfurt – "in the banking quarter" – he was beat up, him, sixty-eight years old! But since he had *once* learned judo, he would *always* be able to defend himself. Even this time, when he was already on the ground and those guys were stomping on his thighs: "It's a lot of fun, you know, jumping around on somebody's thighs." But he struck back with the hard edge of his hand and knocked one of the guys off, laying him straight out on the ground. "Then I got it in the nose. Not that I'm trying to make any excuses for my nose, and I already had these bags under my eyes, too, before I got smacked in the face." It is one of the bad habits of these miserable, used up emcees that they spend much too much time talking about themselves, and they always begin their little tales with *I*. The salesman was acting like one of these characters, and the two ladies hesitated, a little embarrassed, before they politely giggled. But, as he continued to perform, undaunted, it gradually became more and more clear: this wasn't even his own routine, he wasn't even the *I* here, it belonged to some entertainer he was being forced to imitate, not someone on television now, no, it was a voice from the past; maybe the voice of a comedian from one of the stages at the front, one he had heard in his hour of peril, for the first and the last time, a voice he had heard *once* and *since then* could not get out of his mind. And since he had already appropriated this comedian's *manner*, it was not particularly difficult to manufacture similar jokes of his own. So it was, that there was almost never a beating in his life he couldn't beat with this wit. But suddenly, in a minute observation that sounded untrue in a way different from all the rest, his duality, the split, flared open. Actually there had been two people, "me and my sales representative," on that business trip to Frankfurt. He had let this man take the first taxi at the stand, and while he was waiting for the next one, he had been attacked. Anyone who believes this will be saved, the two old ladies smiled gently.

. . .

In the office building across the way, the lights on the fourth floor are burning brightly late into the night. They are celebrating a birthday. Employees whose well-manicured fingers normally pass around papers and computer reports to each other are now in each other's arms, swaying back and forth together, or dancing in the confined space which is still packed full of the stench of their work.

. . .

Once more, exactly like last year, a birthday is being celebrated across the way on the fourth floor of an office building. How in the world can anyone hang around in his office until one o'clock in the morning, when this is the place he has to come back to early the next morning and sullenly set himself back to work? That's just it! They'd like to make a filthy mess of the very desk on which they otherwise do nothing but shove around nice neat reports.

. . .

A distracted glance into the heart. In a café, a young woman is writing a letter. When she looks up from time to time, I am sitting, as it turns out, in her direction. When she is thinking something over and raises her head, there, where she is seeking her thoughts, are my eyes, and she looks out into the lens of my glasses.

. . .

On top, when we smile, we both sexes still have the same chances. Down below are the inequalities of the body, the one disparity. But, since smiling represents the highest level of social achievement our dumb bodies are capable of . . .

I once met this young girl. A little overwhelmed by her beauty, I began looking off to one side, or down at my own hands. I let her speak, for almost three hours, and I listened as she aired what were purely her own unseasoned views, lively, simple-minded, and spoiled, remaining completely unaware of what she was actually doing. I found out that to a wonderfully beautiful twenty-year-old, there is nothing of greater interest in this world than her own well-being and enigmatic fluctuations. Just this past week, her consciousness had been raised enormously, all of a sudden and for no discernible reason. Even yesterday, she had made her way through the supermarket singing to herself. From a distance of almost twenty years, one views the more recently born as a princess sleeping on a pea. One nods, one smiles half-heartedly and can only think: how much I would love to despoil her. This young thing is completely unsuspecting, but the sparkling armor of narcissism is protecting her from seduction, influence, and head-turning, and thus she who can hear so little will never be anyone's slave. Anyone who is sufficiently pleased with herself does not possess the curiosity, actually a concoction of greed, that at this age makes even the awareness of seduction possible. She likes only happy movies. Her professional ambition: to become a film director; in any case, to have some key position, it doesn't really matter where. She reminds me of a cold queen in a Buñuel film. And she says: "Buñuel? Never heard of him."

When she called me, it was unmistakable: she's got something she doesn't have to be ashamed of. A bright laugh on the other end of the line very clearly said: if you could see me, you would never even think of refusing to meet me. . . . Why shouldn't we be able to tell from a voice if someone is self-conscious and intimidated, or spoiled and sought after? I remember that she told me, how, at age fourteen, she had worked out her fondest wish and written it down – a bedtime story, in which she appeared as a "really wonderful girl, not me you see, really beautiful and all the boys thought she was enhancing (!)" . . . A slip of the tongue? A blend of enchanting and entrancing? I suddenly had the feeling that through this gap in her speech I was seeing just how untouched she was. I had to say something, but it only slid off into a silly compliment: that she was truly beautiful, and had absolutely no need to seek beauty in a dream. I blushed as I spoke. She didn't really understand what I had said. Or my lustful, embarrassed face suggested that she might well ignore my remarks. In the end, she invited me to go ice-skating with her. I wanted to see her again and I accepted. But I know that I can't skate any more. Not long ago, five little children had to take me by both arms and pull me off the ice, since I obviously couldn't even stand up on my own.

. . .

In these late April days, it is sunny and already as warm as summer. The real estate agents are coming into the pub with their ladies, pre-colored in the tanning salons. One of them sits down with his companion, very sweet-assed, at a far corner of the table. But he hangs her coat on a hook behind my chair. As he is returning to his seat, he quietly says to me, sitting by myself at the mating site of the world of couples: "Okay, you'll help me keep an eye on the coat, won't you!" Is that the way I really look! Like someone they can appoint guardian of the coatrack for this stinking pack, this gang. And then think they're doing me a favor, tossing a few crumbs of spring's amour my way by involving me in a intimate relationship with this adorably common beauty, Christa Kallipygos. She is wearing a dark mink, the blackest of black mink.

. . .

Mother, daughter, and her colleague from work, at dinner, trying to understand why they suffer from such an excessive but entirely cheerless eating obsession. The daughter says: There's nothing she can do. Sitting eight hours in an office, evenings too tired to exercise, then eat, then television, eating some more: Snacking! Huh. It's normal living. She and her colleague had already gone to a spa together, lots of exercise there, diet too, but well, within a year they'd gained it all back. Well. It just can't be helped, it's normal living. They know better, but they always eat too much. Illness? Yes, illness too. Feet. Heart. Just too little exercise. Her deskmate (at the office of the county registrar) says: A year ago had such a whale of a gallstone taken out, but that wasn't really from overeating. Otherwise she's not complaining. I sit down somewhere and I start eating. Well, stuff down half of it. We've got good intentions, keeping it off, keeping it off! I come home at night and both of my parents are eating a lot, I can't just sit there and not eat, then they say: Come on, eat, it's so good, it tastes so good, and we don't want any leftovers, do we! I know that if I were on my own, I could do it, I could get back down under 150 pounds like I did at the spa, I was on a diet there. But together, at home, or with you here, I just can't do it. My mother keeps saying: Keep it off, keep it off, but it's so hard. Once, twice, my God, I can take it off, but keep it off!

This is what we hear them saying during dinner, incessantly tormenting themselves with talk about the dangers of excessive eating. Squeezed into an unfriendly habitat, plagued by crazy, one-sided ideals of beauty, ridiculed by the lean majority in their environment, cursed by their doctors in the name of a questionable diet science, these fat eaters lose every trace of what might be called joyous or robust. Their excess, their gluttony lacks all splendor and expression of power. They sneak something forbidden and fall into an absolutely cowering posture. Instead of standing up and displaying their abundance, their broad forms, which fit so well with desire and pride, they hunker down over their tables and lose themselves in self-contempt, which is only interrupted now and then by a shot of indifference, a shrugging of shoulders, ah, what's the difference if we let another dumpling roll onto our plates. It tastes so good – but we don't really enjoy it.

. . .

The costume designer L. is talking about her trips to New York and Tokyo. But what she's really working through is the question of where women working in the arts get their inventive energies ("creativity"). She says that her mother had her first child at the age of twenty-two. This child, according to the mother, had robbed her, the mother, of her own childhood, extinguished it. But from that time on, she no longer had any phobias about going into government offices, or going shopping. Up until then, these phobias toward unknown authorities had always been with her, and even as a married woman she would turn into a child when she had to do as much as stand across the counter from store clerks, who in our times have almost nothing in common with the greedy affairs of the open marketplace. But for her, every man *behind* a store counter was a secret owner, proprietor, simply a powerful person whom one had to ask for something. Every time she paid, it was as if she were turning over hot treasures saved, and not the cool, liquid means of exchange she had earned working in an office.

In one fell swoop, the child freed her from such debilities, but, as it seems, had also snatched her own childhood away, as the mother explicitly confessed to the daughter, L., in later years.

Robbing someone of her childhood, L. thinks, is the same thing as cutting memory off from its source of nutrients. And without memory there is no creativity. At that moment, I didn't know what to say; but L.'s concise conclusion led me to more extensive reflection and would not let go of me for some time. It occurred to me how, whenever women (were they always mothers?) told me anything about their childhood, I was often overcome by an exaggerated sense of reluctance, even gloomy boredom. Not only were their stories for the most part pale and lifeless, what they lacked most of all was that trembling lustful ache with which a human being calls back what has been lost, they lacked that excitement, or that pained point of bringing back to this moment, which enables another person, a listener, to take an interest in the *whole* person of the storyteller, since he can hardly involve his imagination in some fleeting sentimental detail out of a stranger's past. Women who have remembered their past in my presence have not done so in the maelstrom of real loss. Of course, their memory of this and that, from back then, was quick and precise – and maybe that was just it: they had a memory *of* something, they did not remember and they did not recall – and it turned out to be nothing more than a flat, rather anecdotal mention, unfomented, without fundament and flow.

Have we really robbed women of their powers of memory? And is it the children they bore who did it?

In their mature years, men established a more or less vast capacity to remember. In the case of women, little of this capacity seems to have developed, or reemerged. In the traditional family, where almost all of the responsibility for upbringing and care of the children was hers, she had to keep looking straight ahead, while from all sides every last bit of available selflessness was demanded of her, a situation that in the meantime has been sufficiently criticized in a changed social order, and in part even abolished, of course acknowledging the fact that certain emotional claims and more profound prejudices cannot be so easily pushed aside. The selfless being was, of necessity, also the being without a memory, and only the egocentric remember with intensity. Far from allowing a child to touch his childhood, in a son, more than in a daughter, a man possesses the material for wondrous self-contemplation. I can still remember with what strange desire my father, through fierce dictate, attempted to implant in me, his son, his early memories, his times lost. I could pass an exam about *his* youth. I had to tell him how *he* built rowboats with his brothers, how his strict father punished *him* the first time he came home drunk. These were intensely authoritarian memories and I often had the feeling that he was using them to win me away from the maternal world of nurturing and everyday reassurances, and I was supposed to accompany him back into *his* past, where we would both be happier. His memories were seldom dulcet and tranquil; they were most often rebellious. They were too overwhelming for him to control. They were circumstances, convulsions, of what had once been in confrontation with the chains of a narrow, poor, ripe life, which had met all expectations in one way or another. They were no doubt combined with a reaction against his life circumstances. And through the despotic temperament of paternal memory, the unformed child experienced early on, too early, criticism and a sense of the inadequacy of his own reality, whose wealth of temptations he had just begun to explore. He also learned about the energy needed to disagree, to recognize inadequacies, in order to creatively struggle against them. In the beginning of reflective criticism, longing and memory, hope and homesickness, were still fused together in one fiery core. Only later did a cooling rationality separate the elements of a socially enlightened belief in progress from those of an irrational, "sick" longing to return – perhaps never a valid separation.

Thus, memory was not only a technique of masculine creativity, but also a privilege of masculine predominance in the family. The spirit of their heritage was primarily presented by the father.

But in so many of these biographies, wasn't there a grandmother, an old storyteller, who first gave depth to a child's hour and served up the past in full measure? Weren't the Old Women the ones who remembered? Apart from the fact that growing up in a rump of a family here, in this country, only very few of us ever had a storytelling grandmother, many of the stories they told were more often handed down than experienced, and they lacked the subjective emphasis, the "sickness" born of sorrow, with which my father remembered the "best years of his manhood."

L. said: today, when I hear my mother and her sister, both of them over seventy, and now back together again after each survived her husband – what do they remember about their girlhood? How scratchy the wool socks were. Where they had their best vacations. But they disagree about this, whether it was at one aunt's home or the other. They don't tell any stories. Back Then is not the fundament of their lives. Their memories only scratch the surface, catch only the cuff of a wool sock – where an entire continent of eroticism has slid down, sunk, become packed away under ice.

. . .

For a woman, there is no "Last Volume." For a woman, there are only "Happy Days." Eternity is the realm of women. "Another heavenly day!" they say, when there is little more than half of their lives left on this earth.

That is the way things once were. How will it be in the future when mothers begin to remember?

. . .

Pina Bausch, a legend of purity. Perhaps rather flat, but monotonous right up to the clarity of despair, in this dance theater we can see: how this supposedly most natural of realms still left to humankind, the pure mating act is simply teeming with fake faxes and forms, numbers and styles, with *society*. There is no fulfillment for those who are perpetually aroused.

Human sexuality is a Sisyphead, a dream of impotence. It is continuously striving toward the high point of *nature*, toward which it is luring us with the power of promised reconciliation. Yet, the wretched shall never be granted the experience of this high point: they will never reach it. Except maybe in something like that short, half-second-long muddying of consciousness at the rollover of orgasm? And if, as most often is the case, joyous ecstasy is not achieved, if things fall two centimeters short of bliss? Happiness sets its own standards and measures its own values, the relative is always there and acknowledges no high point. And thus the ringing laughter of the devil, who, according to ancient word, mocks us after every act of intercourse.

No, no matter how free we try to make it – outside of love! – we will always remain social creatures, and, as long as we *make love*, we will continue to mass produce cultivated beings. *Ars amandi* or *Joy of Sex*: we cannot escape the forms, the values, the rules of a total culture. And furthermore, it is certainly more satisfying to approach lovemaking with perfectly formed comprehension rather than burdening it with a ferocious desire for *pure* sexuality, which, in the image of its madness, only love itself can fulfill.

. . .

Message from a Cambodian man to a woman, before he is executed by the Khmer Rouge:

"I love you but you will never know it.
For you are a star, and I am only
an earthworm and I will be crushed."

For dust is dark and fate has denied me the pride of a brave warrior who goes to a death worthy of your love. As a victim, as one who was dragged away from his house, I am so vanishing and meaningless that you would not even recognize me in a line of victims. I am ashamed that I, your husband, am such an unknown and a random target of the enemy's killing machine. My death is a miserable and inexcusable offense in the grand and boundless history of our love. You, survivor, are over me forever; to this nothing, this earthworm, you appear like a star. The star will never know the love of the nothing. Still, it is eternal, for this message possesses the almighty power of being the last thing a man has said.

. . .

A film about a housewife who is dying of a brain tumor. The story of a cancer patient, portrayed by a prominent actress, dispenses with every attempt at shielding our emotions, dispenses with trendy effects like consciousness-raising by shorting all emotion, and dispenses with the slanderous regard for a doctrine of social salvation we have come to know sufficiently well from television films, totally trashy in terms of their aesthetic morality and modes of expression. Here, the greatest of mankind's catastrophes is squeezed through the needle's eye of "what social conditions caused them to come about," and then they are allowed to trickle away on a slender thread of ephemeral consolation. But there was nothing in this film that would allow us to escape an immediate and personal struggle with our feelings. In silent, head-on, emotional turbulence, the play of illness, as if from antiquity, unfolded in a procession of catastrophe and inevitability, along with the terrible tricks of hope – an anonymous drama that had pressed its mask of terror onto the friendly and helpless faces of an ordinary Swedish family. The strange thing about all this: to sense the shock, fear and dread of a *viewer* as the purest of anti-sexual stimuli – or is it really just the opposite: the most profoundly consexual? As a viewer, to experience how a human being dies through herself, the crying, the touch, the depth fulfilled, the last – is that not what we expect from a radical embrace, the actual *essence* of sexuality, the sorrow of desire? But such a powerful emotion can only bring us pain, not joy, a feeling we are involved with on a so much more superficial basis. The death of another person, miserable, innocent, everyday, is our entire heart. We desire this person in suffering, we have an erection in suffering. This person dies and we have an orgasm of pain, convulsion, and inundation. All really true desire seems to be an emanation of this central feeling for death. Even happiness only has value when we sense: it does not come from on high; it only lifts us up two feet above quivering emptiness.

. . .

"Only us," *sada kichizo futari*/Sada and Kichizo, only us: this is what the prostitute in Oshima's film *In the Realm of the Senses* carved into the left thigh of her murdered lover. She had strangled him while they were making love and then cut off his penis and his testicles. For four days she wandered around Tokyo in euphoric madness, wearing her lover's genitals around her neck. "Only us" is the name of this grand story. And to the extent that without decorative plot it envelops us in a test of radical love, in that of our own corrupt sexuality, which, between casual consumption on the one hand and domestic frustration on the other, is always fleeing its essence, it is an uncompromising lesson in desire. When Sada and Kichizo, the prostitute and the master, put themselves in a place, a state, and an hour of annihilating Love-Isolation, they remind each of us of the Day-Break of being in love, whenever that may have been, and the boundless promise of the First Round. What seems extreme in the film is known to each of us as the exhilarating initiation of a grand encounter: being exclusive, the true asocial, i.e., ecstatic rebellion against the mediocre concerns of the everyday and work, upon which the permanent hide-and-seek of love bodies and time-consuming desire work their sabotage. Still, for most of these sufferers the First Round represents the outer limits of their addiction. Everything that follows, wanes. Ecstasy does not survive introduction into social existence. Even though this existence actually produced it, making use of the antisocial lure of passion in order to tightly tie down one more particle. But *In the Realm of the Senses*, a kind of generator rules, one that uses physical friction to continually produce new streams of desire, a constructivism of lust which knows only growth, escalation, and excess. It remains a hermetic, asocial ritual, there is no reckless play involved here, no memory, no irony of stimuli, even if in the beginning, the man, Kichizo, must often laugh about the power of incessant desire, even if Sada's *familiar* grin of greed never leaves her lips until the very end. In the isolation of lust there is no perversion, no friction with external objects, none of the dirt of any distraction, no biology, and finally no food, no dreams, no work; the purism of the sexual exchange is total. And since no other living being on earth possesses the autonomy and natural facility for such sexual waste, the film is at the same time an elementary lesson in a fundamental dilemma of the human species. The lust for perpetual lust is simply a construct of the senses, and does not in reality create a balanced system in which the act of love would find fulfillment in endless repetition. Even here, the end is the motor of all things. It may well seem that love and greed are striving toward extreme impasse, where only death, the absolute consumption of the sensual prey, is the ultimate escalation, but in truth this death is an aspect of the first overwhelming encounter that takes place between the two of them, and the labor of radical (as opposed to socialized and diminishing) love consists of nothing but the unrestrained and true fulfillment of the First Moment.

Apart from that, over the course of their unions, Sada and Kichizo do not become more alike. Although the purity of greed remains unclouded in both cases, in the end it does seem that the woman's love is more powerful, even without the egocentric and vengeful, the maenadic triumph. She is the one who strangles the man at the height of his rapture and castrates him, but he surrenders himself, basically without resistance, to this transgression, he allows himself to be led into the room and the ecstasy of this single act; of course, we learn nothing more about this last male obsession, to be sacrificed, and all that is left is the expressionless cadaver; while, in Sada's rapture, consummation robbed of the senses is made visible. Still: at the end as well as the beginning, it was not the victory of one over the other, but the victory of love over time.

. . .

As art, Oshima's film is the work of a reductionist who, like Krapp with his tape recorder, is hunched over the endless event, the One Muscle of Lust, the endless memory of a single incidence of lust. But something essential differentiates this reduction of lust from the departure from all lust. While "case three, reel five" contains everything, in *words*, that can be said, and hardly needs expanding upon, the harsh, un-saying routine of the senses has a fierce inducement to speak *about* the senses to us, and through what is said we seek to bridge the painful fissure we see, namely, that our sexuality is ready for something which cannot be survived.

. . .

In contrast, an original discovery in the relationships market, from the lowlands of erotic reality. The beauticians' instructor and the Persian. The platinum blonde hair would like to lure the coal black hair into a solid, steady relationship. She does not hesitate to explain that she will still have to "test" him beforehand. The Persian writes short stories ("the story you are in"), but the woman, grasping and smiling distractedly, cool and splendidly made up, wearing a stone gray silk vest, pays no attention at all to what he is saying. When the test person asks her about the reason for her silence, she says: "I am like Old Shatterhand, my face is very calm when I'm thinking, I could even say, almost dumb." As far as she is concerned the needs of the writing Persian are elementary, and he will not be disillusioned, either by the arrogance, or the love-deadening dullness of his dream woman, who broadcasts dumb sayings along with bad breath. She has already decided she wants to live with him. She is considering whether or not to get her own apartment, even though she is still married. If she had an apartment, he could come over tonight, for example: "I have a need to see you . . . really see!" she says, with intimate emphasis. But this was only a precipitous, though necessary, declaration meant to arouse, and then the test is immediately resumed with a report on all sorts of details and unshakable facts about her family life. "There are some things I just delegate to my mother. I delegate. Errands that I should do, I have her do them. For example, my mother-in-law has been wanting this Christmas present for years. But it's too expensive for me. But my mother sees this thing on sale somewhere, and so I have her buy it."

From Christmas sales, it is only a small leap to the sudden, rather brazen consideration of whether or not a relationship of the kind she is contemplating with the Persian would really be worth it for her. "Worth it, you know, if it's worth it. You know, we Germans are always asking what we can get out of things, where's the benefit, how am I going to profit from this, personally."

The Persian laughs half intrigued and half amused, and shakes his head a little puzzled. It is not every day that he finds himself in the presence of a woman who is so obviously both this lewd and this straightforwardly greedy. So, what she means is: if I enter into a steady relationship with you, what sort of guarantees will you be offering me, I mean, of a financial sort? She is married after all. But always several steady relationships on the side. "But with Ronald," her husband, "the emotional contact, the feelings, the exchange, the understanding, the tolerance, the mutuality, that doesn't just go away, it can't be erased from one day to the next. Don't think I'd have stayed in a loveless marriage for ten years!"

Of course, several years ago there was a very intense relationship with another man. A man who only really cared about himself, and naturally that made him irresistibly attractive to her. A taxi driver. "Would you like to hear about it?" Well. She was coming out of her cosmetician's class. Waiting for a taxi. One drove right by, the pig. The next one stopped. She gets in. She starts talking to the man. They have an animated discussion. She gets out in front of her apartment building. So does the taxi driver. They talk for a while longer at the front door. Finally, she says that she thinks their conversation is so interesting, that if he feels like it he'd be welcome to come upstairs for a while. But she did want him to know that her husband would be there waiting for her. He said that wouldn't really be a problem, he would call his wife on the taxi radio, and invite her to join them. So, the four of them continued the conversation in her apartment. The two of them, "my husband and I," didn't really get along all that well with the wife. And then things took their course. It was not at all difficult for him to get her into his grasp. Things developed. The listening Persian: "And then one day . . ." "And then one day," she chimes in, smiling watchfully. "Everyone did what they could to see that we were alone as much as we possibly could be. It lasted five years. So you see: I have always been in steady hands."

. . .

(In the past) nothing but a predatory concept of woman. She had to be wrested away from someone's possession, the family's, another man's, or even from innocence.

(Today) we find ourselves in total agreement. New lies of the censorship of passion, new game rules for repression. The hysterical woman of what has become a murky freedom is no more surefooted than the repressed victim of a bogus bourgeois morality. A young woman stands up, screams, and hits the guy, her boyfriend, hard, twice over the back of the head with her handbag, and then runs out of the pub. Her girlfriend moves down two stools away from the pale boy, now leaning over his beer glass, grinning tensely and embarrassed, and without looking directly his way she keeps banging her hand on the table and bemoaning the state of things in a monotone voice: "What a bunch of shit, just pure shit, it's [not *you're*] just a pile of shit." And so on, always the same old puke. There is something compulsive in these waves of oblique castigation; it almost seems as if she cannot tell the guy off because the words, the only ones he deserves to hear at this moment, are somehow no longer hers to employ.

. . .

The man holds a young girl's pendant between two fingers. "A pretty ornament." "A what?" the teenager asks. "It ornaments you," the man says, and smiles, "it really does ornament you. Decorate... We used to say: 'A wife is a husband's ornament.' " The young girl looks at the pendant and shakes her head incredulously.

. . .

What remained of her, fragments of a foundering erotic sovereignty.

A woman is standing in front of the wall of a building, her right leg bent, foot resting on the wall, knee pointed outward; ready to be ready to defend herself.

A woman is taking your picture, spreads her legs, shoves her pelvis forward, receives you, snapping-castrating.

A woman who, after three silent days of contemplation and hard-hearted self-examination, strikes out and screams: I do not want you! Not you!

A woman runs ten outspread fingers through her hair at the exact moment you are about to embrace her.

A woman startles you from behind with thoughtless hands, pressing her fingers over the lens of your glasses, and asking: Who am I?

A woman points an extended index finger at you, and commands: You! Think!

A woman stops in front of you and then doesn't move an inch. In your affable gaze, she is investigating to what degree your heart may be unfrozen.

. . .

Evening after evening, a taxi stops in front of his window. The driver turns on an interior light and opens the back door. But no one gets out. Instead, her voice rings out through the stereo speakers in the back window, saying: "*C'est tout ce que vous avez, je vous laisse seul, et vous le savez.*"

. . .

You notice how one thing has completely withdrawn and has gradually become Utopian, but you still need it so badly: the seeing human face.

We are being exposed to face-deleting forces. Like sulfuric acid in the air, saturated with poisonous gases, it is eating away at antique columns and marble visages, and in just this way the plague of copied photos, the glimmer of television screens, blowups on billboards, are eating away at the luster of our own vision. Only the luster? Everything of essence, which had once lay in the open eye, has withdrawn: Searching and knowing, trusting and calculation, goodness and greed. We do not see, nor are we seen.

Missing begins when you find yourself going against the crowd, the passersby, the strange faces, and you become aware of how many are unreadable and worn down and easily confused.

And suddenly, more knowing than your closest friend, warmer than your own father in a dull daguerreotype, a stranger looks at you. There it is, in that instant, the seeing face that does not recognize in order to immediately destroy, which holds you and envelops you in its distance, and you know where you will go next, and you will never have met such a face in all your lived life.

Once more, using the simple entrances which lead into a person through voice, walk, and face.

There is no science of the human face. In this field of indisputable signs, the hallucinated whole of a living being obstructs every assessment of detail. Still, we approach another face, the externalized secret, with the tireless urge to know and to assess, at first bringing stereotypes into play, and a highly fantasized mixture of fractions of the similar and generalized, in our attempt to see through it, and then we swiftly draw our conclusions as to the traits, the "content" of another person. The face, raised up off the earth over the course of evolution, is not only a human being's most active social organ, it is also the only body part, which, apart from the donning of a mask or a veil, is almost never clothed, it is nakedness, itself, the highest instance, the actual construct of the "unprotected anterior" of upright man. This is why we believe that we can see the undisguised whole of a person in his face, and yet we experience this whole in its most sensual aspect, without being able to grasp it clearly or to interpret it, as inadequately as we can discern the true meaning of a dream without knowledge of its symbolic structures. The face, to the extent that it is the external radiance of the soul, is always a mysterious veil of faces. When we meet a stranger, and talk about this encounter at home, we rarely mention anything about the face of the other. It is as if we are obeying an intimate taboo, when we express ourselves extensively about the sympathy or antipathy we feel toward another human being, but remain silent about the immediate source of our emotions. Our descriptions of a face are usually limited to the roughest of generalizations: a nose was large, the eyes were piercing, etc. Only very rarely do we admit to being concerned that our opposite's front row of teeth was kept from view; a stiff, narrow upper lip kept it tightly under wraps during the entire conversation; and now we are totally convinced of this man's toughness and natural authority. How difficult it would be to give an appropriate depiction and evaluation of the frequency of changes of expression, of mien, which are the source of all effect. We generally hesitate to draw any conclusions about the character of a person based on external features ("over which he has no control"). And we are well advised to do so, especially when we consider the fundamental failure of the physiognomists, from Aristotle to Lavater to the anthropometric experiments in the Third Reich, all of whom drew the wrong conclusion from a valid observation. Then, how can we make appropriate use of a valid observation without letting it deteriorate into a erroneous theory? A face must be read like a dream; a face *is* the dream language of every encounter. A far-reaching act when one human being looks, a far-reaching echo when another smiles. Also a far-reaching field of radiation: the endless shadings of being estranged in an eye beholding you. The deeply grounded caution and the elementary mistrust, which always protect the eye, us in our most extreme nakedness, while the mouth, the fingers, the entire body have long since gotten over the basest aspects of self-consciousness. Eyes and the way they function are certainly more than a psychoanalytic symbol for the genitals. In this More there is curiosity, there is a logic of discovery which attracts and evades, which seems to constantly force a rational analysis of the face, only to steer this analysis brusquely back into the realm of the imaginary.

. . .

It is remarkable, even embarrassing, how, the older we get, the more we tend immediately, almost compulsively, to form an image of another person's essence, even though our contact is fleeting. The fluidum of the way a finger is held, the countenance of a walk, and the powers of our so-called "experienced inference" (Heidegger) are activated, and this, along with the help of a few observations, a few bytes of sense data, allows us to swiftly project the entire range of another's behavior, often we even feel an inner compulsion to do so, and quickly work out any number of possible situations in which we have an authentic view of this person, the way he stands, the way he speaks.

The arrogant intelligence of a university professor, late thirties, a *Tageszeitung* reader, whose highest aim it is to be able to speak, nonstop ("just like the empty-headed rest of the world") about motors, excellent restaurants, fantastic places to take a vacation. "The latest tests are now out for a car model that easily puts 250 horsepower out on the street." One look, one overheard sentence contains so many particles, and so many multiples of particles, of his being that it is actually possible to see, in one and the same instant, how this man uses a nail file, or to hear how he answers when his wife calls him a liar.

. . .

The young judge who is trying to hide his lack of self-assurance from the defendant. Making an impression of being far too nice, he keeps alternating between his shy, boyish laugh and a staid and surly mien. It does not suit him, he has to shake it off. Wrinkled forehead, a turn of the head, then immediately back to the obligatory, seemingly witty, in truth entirely affected laugh; always the anxiety of not being able to figure out quickly enough what is at issue, not asking the right questions, not looking intelligent, making some little procedural misstep, not looking like a sovereign upholder of the law.

• • •

Couples of various ages, indestructibles from solid academic circles, meet every Monday for dinner in their favorite pub. The leader of the pack, the one who sits at the head of the table, a surgeon about sixty, always ready to joke around, grabs the young wife of a colleague by the arm in order to guide her to a seat, nonchalantly squeezing her upper arm at about breast level, with the suggestively physical contact always allowed cavaliers of the old school, soon shifts his attentions to the waitress, twinkling gold tooth, refers to the casserole as a battleship. His gaze immediately frosts over whenever it by chance comes to rest on his own wife. The wife seems older than her age, very gaunt, narrow bony face, thick glasses, the embodiment of a Protestant minister's daughter possessing values, takes her lorgnette out of her handbag in order to study the menu, after some hesitation orders a glass of rosé, a sign, as it were, that she cannot decide between extremes, between red and white, good and bad, hate and love, she chooses the mixed middle way; gazes, hardly or not at all involved in the conversation dominated by her husband, in a strange, angularly nervous way, always skipping along the same visual pathway, into one of the faces nearby, then at the table again, and quickly into another face, back at the table, and so on, her head bobbing around in a birdlike staccato. This emaciated woman first rushed up to a chemist colleague, somewhat shorter than she is, and selected a sort of compressed greeting, where with teetering gait one approaches very near to another body, completely avoiding the free extension of the hand while drawing the hand of the other, with one's own arm lying flat, elbow bent, almost boldly to oneself, almost to one's own breast. Standing next to her, the daughter of the chemist, waiting to be greeted in similar fashion, tall and gangly, mid twenties, treading from one shoulder to the other, in a calf-length suit skirt, bulky napped tweed, large tear-shaped glasses, just this past June put the bar exam behind her, in "jurisprudence," as her father puts it, ugly in the sense that all her law cleverness seems to have completely disheveled her, as if the intellect had demanded the sacrifice of her body in order to develop itself; short, sneering laugh, as if she were seeing through something that was already obvious to everyone else; her head half bowed and turned to one side, always in possession of her subject, her iron will, and her highbrow renunciation always on display. It might be interesting to imagine her as a judge in a divorce case, where she is removed from the trial for lack of judicial temperament – proven lack of human temperament, proven ignorance of sexual subject matter – "Do you have any idea at all what is at issue in this case?" One might also imagine how, profoundly distressed, she rushes into the judge's chamber, suddenly breaking out in tears, she rummages through the law books, which, taken all together, threaten to come crashing down on her, crushing her into one, single, flat legal loophole.

. . .

No matter who we come together with, at some time we know this person. We are astonished how, step by step, the other (never us, of course) behaves more automatically. From this proximity, we can no longer clearly recognize his essence, but in return, we can more clearly see into the network of drives and the malfunction of drives, of motives and sham motives, for with age the inner scaffolding does not simply shine shyly through any more. We look on rather timidly and think unforgivingly: not much more hull and skin on him, hardly any sign at all of capricious phenomena, what has happened to the unforeseen and to autonomous activity? The wire web of the psycho-puppet, not unlike the skeleton man, has emerged from under the honest derma and taken the place of the independent player. Frightening, sometimes, how little form is left, and how transparent at those worn-down spots the external appearance is, there where – much used – beauty, impact, and will once were.

traffic flow

I looked out of the car window, and in a crowd of passersby just making its way across the intersection, I saw my dear N., with whom I had – once! at that time! back then! – traveled along the same road for a good three years, I saw her walk across the street and head in the direction of a pub. Her head, the part in her brown frizzy hair. She is the same woman I waited for so anxiously in the valley of Pefkos on Rhodes, when, beginning at opposite ends of the road, we approached each other over the rocky hills, and when she didn't appear, and she didn't appear on the horizon, I was so worried that someone might have jumped her from the side of the road and assaulted her. She is the same lover. Caught sight of in half profile, fleetingly, as she was walking along and I was driving by. To me an ungraspable law, that turns someone so intimate back into a stranger. Damn the world of passersby!

. . .

We met clever H. in an Italian restaurant, and there followed perfunctory greetings, a healthy, cleansing session of small talk, and then onto more elevated themes. From this, one would soon have gathered the impression that thinking people today are often the most distracted, that their thoughts come to them only in a tormented state of *flight from thought*, and thus are doomed to be lost. So many precipitous judgments served up in such a short time, so many distinguished names simply tossed around, used to provoke, and add to one's own sheen. And in the meantime, hardly a one of these troubled heads ever asks a question; in an almost agile panic, they avoid the exposure an inquiring person must confront. This also applies to H., who even accepts into the torrent of his opinion the basic Heidegger concept that inquiry is the piety of a thinking mind. So, our conversation ranged from Savonarola to Tàpies and onto Stanley Kubrick, from Rousseau to Carl Schmitt. Finally, a heartfelt farewell from H. He, the pedestrian, heads off in his short-strided gait toward other worries; we, another friend and I, get into my car. Shortly after that we meet H. again as he is crossing the street at a green light. When I catch sight of him, I head straight for him, just for fun, and don't hit the brakes until I'm actually rolling up to his legs, raising my hand to greet him again. But he, not recognizing me behind the wheel, shakes a threatening fist in my direction, the way pedestrians are wont to do when confronted with rude and thoughtless drivers. We have just scaled such intellectual heights together and he doesn't even see me here in traffic, blinded by the external difference in our status, and for him I am nothing more than a piece of hard metal with a rude chauffeur who has almost knocked him, the weak, little passerby, right off his feet. And he shakes his fist at me, looks me in the eye, his devoted friend, and trains his harsh glare on the unknown driver. And even once he gets on his way again, not the slightest shadow of recognition falls across his senses. Of course, it was only a silly mistake; but still a stroke of alienation that will not completely go away.

. . .

The Man Of course, you know Weißtalallee, this broad traffic artery on the south side of the city. That's where she was standing, my beloved, on one side of the street, and I was on the other. She was intending to come over to join me, there was a steady flow of traffic between us and no prospect of a break. In the meantime, she had already taken one step out onto the street, onto the stripes that mark the parking area. So she was standing over there and waiting for a lull in the traffic, all the while paging through a magazine. Then a car started to move into the parking space; exactly where she was standing. I can remember it very clearly, it was lime green, one of those Citroëns whose owners had it painted lime green (they don't come in lime green any more). But what does it mean, to park? He pulled up ahead of her, and then back, just to make sure she could see him. The guy behind the wheel wanted to get noticed, by the woman I love, and that was it, nothing more. But when she doesn't look up, at him and his remarkable lime green, he actually starts to pull into the parking space, backs right up to her, pulls up a little, then back – but he misjudges the distance. And when he backs up, he hits the woman whom he wants to impress in the knee, she falls right down onto the ground. You know how ridiculous it looks, how dismaying it is, when a well-dressed person you love falls down on a public thoroughfare . . .

The man in the street spoken to and pulled aside Oh, yes. You know, something a lot like this happened to me once. But it was at Lake Wörther . . .

The Man She is lying on the ground, more scared than injured, I believe. The guy jumps out of the Citroën; it began as a flirtation, it became an accident. Instead of smiles, winks of the eye, and flattery, only rolling eyes and coarse invective. He lifts my beloved up off the street and they start screaming at each other – he screams, too, the accident transformed the person once desired into a little piece of aggravation. And you see, I am standing on the opposite side of the street, while over there – on the far bank, I almost want to say – someone has done something to her, and even if she hasn't been injured, she was knocked down into the dirt. Right in front of my eyes she fell out of the quiet and relaxed pose in which I, so full of expectation, had been observing her from the other side of a flow of traffic which would not let up. She lay in grotesque disarray in the gutter, a smashed statue made of marble or clay has more appeal and remnants of dignity in its thousands of shards than does a beloved person, knocked down, completely stupefied and made physically a fool. I must admit that, for a moment, in spite of my outrage, I was overcome by a sensation of cold, and I, on my side of the street, stopped desiring her. For the first time, I felt how it was not to love her.

The man on the street spoken to and pulled aside Yes, yes! You're right, you're right!

The Man And the guy gets back into his Citroën and speeds off. My friend . . . my wife looks at me across the traffic and just shakes her head. Yes: all she does is shake her head, after all that! And not even in a way that would indicate utter bewilderment, no, only a brief, little shake, the kind that seems to say "What does he think he's doing!" Seen through my eyes, a totally inadequate gesture after this perilous incident. She is not at all aware of her entire fall *in my eyes*. She's already looking at her magazine again, though it is now somewhat sullied by dirt from the street.

The man on the street spoken to and pulled aside When it happened to me, I was standing very much like that in front of the post office in Velden . . .

The Man Oh, please no: don't start telling me the same thing about yourself, and not even anything you have suffered remotely resembling this. It has cost me enough energy to talk about this for the first time. In case you don't find anything incomparable in my story, then I must still beg you to please keep quiet, out of heartfelt sympathy. Spare me your parallels, and do not shove this man, looking out from his lonesome vantage on the edge of the street, down into the phenomenon of the frequent of any man who might be standing there. Otherwise, with all the strength I have, I would have to tear back out the trust which I so carefully let flow into you, whom I do not know, and with whom I have had nothing but a casual exchange. So, please be quiet and keep your parallels to yourself!

. . .

The fat carcare fanatics, Sundays on the edge of the street, bending way over into the engine compartment, squatting down alongside the door to take care of a scratch, and jeans together with underpants slip way down over hairy rear ends. Why bother with pants, shirt, and shame on the street if you're so ready to bare your ass in front of your car, your lover?

. . .

An old married couple at a busy intersection. The man is leaning on a barrier that is meant to keep pedestrians from crossing the street on the far side of the traffic light. He is staring down at the street, at the asphalt surface, leaning on his arms, his hands folded in front of him, as if he were viewing from on high a beautiful landscape, or the shimmering course of a river. Next to him his wife, in a similar attitude with her gaze directed at the same evocative spot. A streak of mother-of-pearl on a papilla bed of raw asphalt. The Walk light turns green. Since no one is crossing, cars begin making their right turns in droves, obliterating the spot without boundaries which had so transported the two old people as one, traversing their inscrutable vista.

. . .

A girl crossing the street in a cream-colored linen skirt imprinted with a carmine red pattern shaped like the rings of a tree trunk.

A girl in a long camel hair coat with a capelike drape, with what looks like a very woolly, sand-colored pair of full-cut flannel slacks, a softly covered, much muffled figure. She is approaching her parked VW from the front, her left side touching the car door. Bending over slightly, at the hips, with her right hand she inserts the key into the lock, and while she's opening the door – for no other reason than posture, not interest – she looks back at the side of the street she has just come from.

Haven't we all looked into a hundred thousand faces? This kind of occurrence is the opposite of a "representative selection": it is the truth state of a physical, linear number. How many people do we come into contact with over the course of a normal lifetime, with how many where words or an extended gaze are exchanged – from our mothers to the many who once may have stopped us on the street to ask for directions?

To be and remain transitory. Every open face and every gait gracefully trod pulls you off course. You trot off after them like a lost dog after the next best master.

. . .

. . . and you merge into the while of another.

A few moments with human beings are filled with affection that will remain incontestable, and we will be able to say: yes, then we were not alone, we came together, we experienced something good. In a single, successful convention there is more happiness than we can bear. These have almost never been moments of physical desire, or lust. The memory itself is tender, a gift of sublimation.

. . .

When you leave the hotel dining room to go to the reception desk, you walk along the middle axis of the building in the direction of a glass door which separates the two spaces from each other. However, for reasons unspecified, this folding door is closed and blocked. The only sign, shortly before you reach the passageway, is for the detour you are to take through a side corridor, a thin yellow arrow pointing the way. Over the course of the evening, guests keep falling victim to the seduction of the main axis, and of the blind certainty that they will always be able to pass through this door, which, after all, consists of almost nothing but transparency, only to be painfully halted from time to time. The ones who try to open the door by pulling on the handle, also made of glass, come away in better shape than those who attempt to propel it open with the inertial force of an unknowing body. A young man approaches with a casually outstretched arm, preparing to gently push the door open, he even smiles and turns his head around as he walks out in front of his companion. The observer, constantly keeping the locked door in sight, anticipates the impact, the shock of sudden constraint that erases the smile from the face – he does run into the door, stumbles, bangs his knee against it; his graceful bearing shaken, the loving contact with his girlfriend rent asunder. He takes a step back, looks as if the almost invisible door has repulsed him like anathema. Now he tries pulling it open, attempting to force his way through with technique and craft, while continuing to play the gentleman who understands how to remove every obstacle which may block a woman's way. But finally, before too many vain efforts cast a shadow of doubt over his sense of the practical, he catches sight of the arrow which points the way around. He smiles again, and the two of them, arm in arm and – it seems – a little bit closer than before, head for the way out along the side corridor.

Three older businessmen approach the door. They are walking together, but each of them seems to be keeping to himself, profoundly lost in thought. From the observer's vantage point things look bad for the first man. He is wearing glasses and does not notice the translucent barrier. So, without an arm outstretched, he runs face first into the glass. His glasses pinch the thin skin on the bridge of his nose. This man has run straight into the door without the slightest buffer of caution. His nose is bleeding, he is holding both hands in front of his face. One of his companions calls the accident to the attention of the closest waiter; he passes the report along and a second hurries to the scene with a first-aid kit. The injured guest is temporarily patched up. Throughout the entire affair, the faces of all three men, even of the one who suffered the injury, remain remarkably calm and collected, without the slightest trace of uneasiness or anger. They look impenetrably serious and old-sad, and all of them seem to be involved in such weighty concerns that not even this shock has been able to distract them from their thoughts.

Beyond the glass door, a young blonde woman, dressed in a black uniform and a little white cocktail apron, was sitting in front of her tobacco stand reading a magazine. She has not once taken even the slightest notice of one single impact this evening. Only an inhuman or a supernatural being could remain so blithely put. At the same time, it was this half obscured, thus doubly alluring, vision that everyone wished subconsciously to brush past; the attractive force of her appearance, which invited all to stride right on through the door, was not entirely free of blame in these grotesque collisions with the locked and folded glass.

. . .

Transitory event on the banks of the Wiesent. In front of us, the narrow waters of Franconian Switzerland have been half dammed up, and the other half has become a narrow strait with rapids and low falls running into a small, dark pool, where it is momentarily deep, only to turn again into a straight and gentle stream. Three children are floating along on a rubber raft, approaching the point where the small river divides, the cliff, but are looking at the only person along the banks, sitting cross-legged on a ledge. Satisfied faces, looking around good-naturedly, sunny holiday in August. Suddenly they run aground; the front end of the raft is caught in one of the buoys marking the dam, while the load-bearing end is being drawn into the rapids. They are turning around, paddling in thin air, the boat is listing, it pitches – the birth of terror on round, tanned faces – they are tipping, they capsize, every last one of them falls out of the boat into the pool below the rapids. In a flash, with no resistance to offer against the unforeseen, a young girl, who had just been smiling in my direction, sinks in over her head. The oldest boy and the girl bob up and down in a bubbling draft, not able to swim or too shocked to do so, they dance around each other in the water, pushing themselves apart. The oldest, without being able to find any footing, pushes and shoves the younger brother and the sister onto the bank, for me to pull them out. It is only at this moment that I leap into action and stretch my arm out to the children. My dream of conceited observation tore open once the head of the young girl disappeared under water, and I joined in, no better than the dumbest or the worst of us would have, just barely able to act. I pulled the girl up onto the bank and helped her onto her feet. Hardly is she standing in front of me before I am enjoying the sweet terror that this brief interlude in her existence has left behind on her young face, I am looking at the slippery, wet clothing adhering to her body, her breasts firm, as if they had been created in danger, and it is as if you had seen a child sink, and you pull this being out of the water in the body of a mature young woman. She immediately expresses her thanks (with the grace of still entirely dazed consciousness) for what she herself calls "rescue." "No! I won't ever go boating with you again!" the older one screams angrily, after managing to get himself and his younger brother safely on shore. Then all three of them run after the renegade boat and manage to catch it at the next bend in the river.

In order to play a game with chance, you must always be able to determine which point of force you occupy in a symbolic field, and what you yourself are secretly contributing: a man sitting on a ledge along the bank, keeping watch here along this slender stream as along waters anywhere, allowing desire to well up; in front of him the point of danger, the falls in the river, the approach of the children with their content and unsuspecting faces – and if they had indeed passed calmly by, I would have had to doubt for the very first time that mishap and destruction are incidents of erotic magic. But here and now, there was again no reason to do so.

. . .

A young woman dressed in white linen slacks, legs full-cut and loose, close-fitting and gauzy around the hips, transforming the protruding edges of her underpants and the shadow of her sex into part of the design, comes panting up the basement steps with a jumprope in her hand, after a fitness session at ten o'clock in the evening. Not one glance, not one greeting, no hesitation, only this sweaty whiff of limbs in training, only the hurried ascent of a narcissism as beastly as it is indulgent, as engaged as it is aloof, as untouchable as it is user-intensive; this training apparatus adorned with flesh, this embodiment of indifference, this recycling plant of a sterile grace, this brand-name product of our decade's indulgence, this chic, omnipresent specimen of the athletic but totally uninvolved being – is this the woman we are supposedly attempting to degrade into a sexual object?

Yes, if *sex* could kill! If it could at least confuse, disfigure, distort, make useless, what has been so miserably accommodated and civilized into emptiness, and if it could only challenge the well-conditioned heart. . . . But wouldn't every physical exchange with her inevitably put us in training for just that *pattern* we'd like to kill?

• • •

The owner of a gasoline station, leaning over his cash register, is arguing with an attendant about an appropriate expression, a phrase no longer in widespread use. The owner: "What do you say when you turn something over to someone, but you don't give it to them, you entrust them with it and you believe that it's safe with them? You turn over some money with—?" The attendant: "In full and complete trust." Owner: "No, not that. You give it with—" Attendant: "To the best of your knowledge." Owner: "No, no. You give somebody the money, you don't make out a receipt, you give it to him hmmhmmhmm!" A customer waiting to pay: "In good faith." Owner and attendant simultaneously: "Yes, of course. In good faith."

These expressions are artifacts of colloquial speech, you have to be able to hear them resonate in your ear in order to use them correctly. We all know the vague uncertainty we sometimes have when we use such clichés and phrases, an uncertainty that tends to parody, increasing and distorting the treasure of our idiom. The loss of these expressions makes us feel cut off from the stream of our linguistic heritage, from those elements that are part of custom and community rather than the product of our own, individual style. "How do *we* say—?" is the way we often begin a question when we're looking for one of these expressions, thus establishing an ironic distance, inserting the quotation marks of collective memory. We ourselves are no longer familiar with the phrase, we haven't heard it for a long time, it doesn't belong to us any more. These days we are more likely to be familiar with the pithy slogans of TV ads. The apprentice gardeners I worked with for a time greeted each other every morning with a gruff "They're still looking for a few good men," but they could have expressed the same disdain by saying: "No rest for the wicked . . ." or "Pick that cotton!"

It is clear that where we do this kind of work together, the excessive use of cliché is all but unavoidable. As a rule, these workplace exchanges seek to establish a common understanding with a minimum of verbal resource. Slang and abbreviated expressions of all sorts come into play. I have never before in my life used "got it" so often, only to sustain the essential flow of consensus, and not to obstruct. In the exchange of opinions, those who toil hard on this earth can afford neither argument nor contradiction. And if someone should happen to object rather than agree, it is simply not passed on. Every instance of speech strives to be common speech, and as such its indirect objective is to express a common opposition and a contradiction of the boss's speech.

. . .

The spirit of interjections. In California, when you thank a salesclerk or a waiter or some other person, instead of "You're welcome," they reply with an unusual abbreviation, an *aahaah*-like tone, but with a half-open mouth and a very high, drawn-out second syllable, nasalized, almost sung. Although it basically means "okay" or "that's fine," to our ear there is something strange in the way it sounds: as if in response to a word of thanks, they are saying "Aha!"

An interjection is the condensed sense of much speech, a feeling word, to put it in terms of school book grammar, which simply slips out of a listener. A *Ha*, *Oh*, *Uh*, or *My God* can reveal a more intimate understanding of another's speech than an expansive response. And what an almost immeasurable wealth of emphasis and allusion can be conveyed by the nebulous particle *hm*. Some of the finest coloratura of sense can only be transmitted through this tiny, supple stub of a sound, from lofty amazement to deepest skepticism, from a muted yes to a surrogate shake of the head, from pleasurably prolonged praise to impatiently accelerated comprehension, basically any emotion can be voiced with *Hm*, depending of course upon the status and the authority of the *Hm*-maker. A person of lower status is usually required to open his mouth a little wider. Of course, in order to be able to give oneself over to the more refined play of voice and temperament, to get everything out of a *Hm* other people use many words to convey, a person must possess a certain measure of sovereignty. And, often enough, it can also be a constricted sound, a sound of concealment, an accentuation of inner uneasiness and a neurotic breakdown of communication. We might be reminded of the nervous "*Hm, Hm*" staccato of peanut-munching Anthony Perkins in *Psycho*, shortly before he rented a motel room to his victim. In the same sense, I won't forget a lost lover's little, willful *Hm* she added to the end of a sentence, or a pronouncement. Was probably supposed to mean: well, that's how things are. Could also have been a sound of the approval she would like to have gotten from others. Not really at ease with herself, an interim-balance *Hm*, a little skeptical, but at the same time a self-administered provocation to keep talking: that's the way it sounded. It simply happened to her, nervous and unaware as she was. Another, equally distracted and nervous tic of a *Hmhm*, always through a closed mouth, out of the throat of a mathematician I once spoke with for a few hours. It always happened when there were extended pauses in the conversation, not unlike a phonetic aftertwitch to a vocal exchange long since accomplished. On the one hand, it seemed to me like the remnant of a stutter otherwise overcome, but it was also like the sound of a deeper, concealed mistrust of one person toward another, an objection. In this case, the imaginary/the subconscious was in fundamental disagreement with what had *really* been said.

Interjections are little, involuntary leaps of emotion in your mouth, and who knows, in the final analysis, maybe all of human speech is nothing but an interjection, a sound thrown into our midst, a feeling word in nature's endless murmur.

. . .

Mother and daughter, both old, since poverty and self-hatred have pressed the same mask of demoralization onto their faces, on a hot summer's afternoon are dragging themselves and an overstuffed shopping bag across an empty church square. The daughter is talking about something in an incessant flow, in a monotone, hardly comprehensible babble. The mother has snapped up a word: "Beasix? What is that? Tea or instant soup?" The daughter, whose speech came to an abrupt halt for the duration of the question, now babbles on, unaffected. Apparently, she's not relating anything, but is only repeating a countless number of brand names to herself. "Beasix is what you said, isn't it?" the mother asks again. "What is that?" The daughter: "I didn't say anything." This is the only understandable sentence she speaks, clear and blunt, and then the babble begins again, the brand-name stream (of wishes) which she cannot grasp, the wares (in the bag) which she cannot grasp – the wares which are out of her reach – the names she cannot keep in mind.

. . .

When quoting prices, the salesclerk has started aping the monotone delivery of a ticket machine, the kind you find in subway stations and parking garages. Her manner just as calm and friendly, she says: "Please pay seven marks and twenty-eight pfennig," instead of "Seven-twenty-eight!" the way most of us communicate this information to each other. A vending machine has become her model of politeness, that is what she mimics.

. . .

In a film like Visconti's *Leopard*, the prince calls his valet to help him on with his jacket, and out from among the theatergoers we hear the stale groan of a young woman of social conscience, and with an "Oh God" or "Uh huh," it's not the film (not even the director's perspective) that's being condemned, only the prince, like the evil character in a puppet show. These idiots of the immediate are no longer capable of acknowledging any kind of distance between the story and themselves, in possession, as they are, of their all-penetrating, see-nothing organs. They immediately make a direct association between themselves and the symbols of the story, they measure everything by the standard of their democratically homogenized, formless social conscience. It is obvious how little power, rage, and direction there is left in protest like this. Nothing but the feeble cycling of a self-satisfied criticism, calcified long ago. When, later in the same film, we hear: ". . . and are currying the sovereign's favor" or something like that, then one of the really young members of the audience is happy. What is a "quadraphonic" brain supposed to make of the term *to curry favor*? The boy has never heard it before. But he's more than ready to snap it up and pin it on his jargon like a new campaign button.

. . .

Preserving the past. Four employees in a music store, among them an older man, probably the department manager, or the store owner, at a welcome party for a new employee. A young woman with a sassy, somewhat lustful face, dark eyes, wiry brown hair, which she is wearing pulled back behind her ears in a style from the thirties. Her contribution to the festivities is a joke well-known among clerks: she characterizes the various social rankings in the company according to film titles. "The apprentices: *As Far as Their Feet Will Carry Them*. The entry-level clerks: *For They Know Not What They Do*. The salesclerks: *Cheated 'til the End*. The management: *The Million-Dollar Thief*," etc. Amazing, to hear this young woman tell a joke from the past, she was much too young to have seen those mostly forgotten movies, or to have had any idea what the films are about.

. . .

A TV-addicted babysitter with her lovely, childlike, punk 'do, the short, spiny hair dyed black, asks the Japanese, Holes-in-the-Belly, if there is anything in his language that is somehow nonexistent in her own German. He tells her about all kinds of peculiarities, but when she notes that he can paraphrase them in German, she raises her hand and brings him to a halt: "Okay, I can see there's nothing that I don't already know about." She is probably fourteen, at the most sixteen years old, has never been to a good school, but *dreams* about getting into a Rudolf Steiner School. When her girlfriend, a good ten years older than she is, once mentions the word "proceeds," the youngster doesn't understand and wrinkles her round brow. "Proceeds," her mother-girlfriend says, "is the money a concert like this brings in." Disgusted, the girl stands up and pages through the program.

. . .

Didn't like the father, didn't like the daughter I heard fighting with each other. She was probably seventeen and wanted more money, he was in his early forties and didn't want to give it to her. The daughter swore at the art professor whose roots were in the student movement, making use of an arrogantly aggressive vocabulary that he himself had once put into circulation, and could still apply today, just not in those instances when he sought to extricate himself from the financial demands of his now-terminated marriage. Between the two of them, the generational conflict had the effect of a tired joke of history, or a serious intermezzo in non-history. All I sensed was: I don't want to know another thing about either one of them. They are both equally in the wrong. And the rest of us are neither for one nor the other, in the same way we are neither for one form of government or another.

. . .

Walked along with them from Wittenbergplatz to Nollendorfplatz, walked along with the homeowners and their friends, alone in the midst of good groupings, many of them couples. Dozens of vans, police vehicles of all sorts, drove us up Kleiststraße. "To Kottbus Gate!" the escaping demonstrators screamed, and some of them took the subway. But no, this is where I have to turn around. I can't just go along with these guys. They are coming at me in droves now that I'm the only passerby headed in the opposite direction. With and without rage against the establishment, a single, uniting passion. Oh, when they get here! the good citizens are thinking, and not only storm the empty houses, but our houses, too, and our apartments and drag us out of our beds . . . ! The building's going to be occupied! Here, grand conjecture has a much greater effect than actual deed. House and home and everything we hold closest are in danger. Not the State, who is that, anyway? But I don't trust any of these hangers-on either, not a one of them! Still: if they didn't exist, if there were no movement, no opposition – then no sense. The outsider sees excitement, significance, something of greater meaning – all the marchers see is corrupt political power. That's why I detest their cheap courage in confrontations with the police; what's anyone got to say when he can no longer sense one square inch of himself, even under the club, only suffering himself to be a fakir of solidarity? Finally, another riot! Just what we need. Too much has remained unravaged over these past few years, redirected into the private sphere. But when we have seen a few not insignificant Enemies of the State become the people's servants, we are no longer overflowing with hope. The next morning, the brusquely cynical remarks of a police psychologist make the paper: "Drop-Outs, Rioters and Co., these are people who have not yet learned to accept their limitations." Here are the police speaking for life's own strategy of disillusionment. No, no we're not going to beat you down to size. Why bother? It's just going to happen to you, anyway. That's life. And haven't too many from your own ranks fallen victim, little by little, to this wretched process, in the end themselves fulfilling the experiential model of the police psychologist? But there are other people, artists for example, who do not lose all courage with youth, but who, as they grow older, become all the more radical and unwavering in the defense of what is theirs. Many a political radical could learn from them how to protect themselves from orthodoxy and leather upholstery . . . Onward, to the Kottbus Gate! Without being part of the movement, you will never learn to think. They'll have to chew their own way out of their suffocating padded jackets.

. . .

Hometown. In my countryside, back home, I went up and down the slopes and across the mountain meadows of the Westerwald, above the narrow valley of the Lahn on whose opposite banks the Taunus mountains begin to rise. Now, behind my parents' home, there is a trail cut through the trees, leading straight up the mountain, a grotesquely cleared stripe running through a child's forest; within its confines a computer-controlled railway that swiftly transports our spa guests out of the city and up into the mountain air, finally delivering them into a grand, new hospital *complex*.

Oh, and I walked by our overgrown land up on the slope, the fence had been torn down, the iron gate broken open, as was the little stone hut, and half burned out. The hut! The one place that always keeps coming back to me, and the sentry of deeper dreams, the hideout from early prohibitions. Neglected, scorched, emptied, sacked, the beginning stands there half open, but I don't want to look inside. The next village lies over the ridge and down the other side of this range. Fog and clouds which retain the snow, and a bloodless blue of the sun. In the former "Imperial City," next to a thousand-year oak long standing beside the flow of the Lahn, this small, serene, almost embraceable body of water with its relentless current, edges, formed in the tension of the small eddies on its surface, sprawled around like long earthworms and dissolved. Later, on the Wehr, at the locks from whose bridges the brave ones among us had leapt off, and during my school years at least two died in this little river, the gentle one, and then contained at the swimming pool – contained? Ah, remembering this seems impossible. The place transformed, overgrown, crumbling – but the *scene*, it is not the one discovered there: the desire, the squirming, the not-daydreaming, the wanting to get to the bottom of things, the same as a quarter century ago. This is the scene in which I told my school friend, while we, having completed our homework assignments, were lying around in our swimming trunks on a warm, free afternoon, keeping watch, that I wanted to philosophize and begin to write an endless book ("about everything"), and so today the least of my writings is not one iota more modest and less demanding than adding another slender thread to the endless weave. The scene endures, the place has crumbled.

Nothing *came into being* here. Here something essential was got hold of, and I can never tire of getting hold of it again and again. My one true experience of time is as a rippling synchronicity. Without the inevitable view of the river (from every window of my parental home) without getting an inescapable concept from the river, I would not have approached the proximity of thinking, and would never have dared to think of the other side of the river, which is one of Not-Passing-By and of Silence.

scribbles

He sat out in the countryside far from any habitation; it was autumn and he was reading a book about the most important thing he had ever read. Soon twilight fell over this scene and then real darkness, and out in the midst of nature, where far and wide there was no artificial light, he struggled to decipher the print, but the book began to conceal itself from him, finally disappearing in his hands and turning black. As this took place, he was never able to reassure himself that he would simply be able to continue reading the next morning at the crack of dawn. He was completely caught up in inexorable withdrawal: blinding – separation – castration.

Until now, *language* alone, he told himself, had made it at all possible for you to endure this immutably miserable isolation. You have no idea what it will be like when once this language demands everything of you, and then fades almost entirely away except for the most ephemeral whoosh. You won't know what real isolation is, until once all that you are able to hear is this most faint rustling somewhere at the outer reaches of your soul. You have no idea how you will sit and cower: words among themselves, but you shut out and incognizant.

. . .

You can find a profound home and a profound exile in language.

. . .

He is often tormented to find that text is not the one, single flame in which all the underbrush of desire can be incinerated. He wants to be text and nothing else. He is ashamed of every other lust. And how he dangles over the abyss when he's at his text, creeping along, exhausted and bitter! It's not that what he's writing is bad, it's that he feels it's bad to write.

. . .

We do not write *about* something, we write *it*; we do not love someone, we love it (love). Love, steel-crowned with the desire for return, with its myth of remelding into one mass of personality. Writing defines the condition of absence. Where there is a single letter, everything is absent. Desire for lost things, the lost body, is the elemental eroticism of a human language that brings about understanding only through sense and symbol, instead of direct stimulation (recognizing, of course, that our cries and our speaking are subject to a behavioral paradigm similar to the one that governs songbirds as they mark off their territory, and stay in continual voice contact with one another).

Signs also have a physical reality, writings are also drawings, are – in part shriveled – things, slender strokes, traces of matter, jewels and secrets.

. . .

Each of us carries the mark of all that has ever been written.

. . .

The crumpled in us,
at night it flattens out, the discarded page with a
bad first line.

. . .

Octavio Paz: "A writer does not speak to us from the national palace, or the supreme court, or from the offices of the central committee; he does not speak in the name of the nation, the working class, the parties. He does not even speak in his own name: the first thing a true writer does is to question his own existence. Literature begins when you ask: who is that speaking inside me when I speak?"

. . .

And Valéry says: "Anonymity would be a paradoxical condition imposed on literary art by a tyrant of the soul. 'In the final analysis,' he might say, 'we have no name within ourselves. Inside ourselves, there are no *they and they*.' "

. . .

We write only in the service of literature. We write under the auspices of everything that has already been written. But we also write to construct, little by little, a spiritual home for ourselves, where we no longer possess a natural one.

. . .

How are we to understand the fundamental triviality of writer and written words? Who are we compared with the mass media and the forces of irrelevance? Nothing now, and never have been. Only when I come to the point of saying, I do not exist and you, written word, only at the edges of a wavelike movement that causes me to dive, do I allot us our appropriate places. The bobbing head of a drunk in an onrushing current, gurgling at the threshold of a scream and sinking back into the waters – this is the fading of a work of art, and, what we seize as it escapes forms the core of its realism. Unimportant: in the meantime all books have lost mass. The realized, complex, enigmatic, insofar as the "inner marketplace" even allows it to emerge, has as little chance of finding fertile soil in which to take root as does the gentle and popular hit of the season. And opposing forces can hardly be maintained where nothing has been developed in the first place. Together, all of these works fall victim to the supreme rule of speed, increasing acceleration, and total passage. If Paul Virilio is right, in the dromocracy (a system based on forces of acceleration) in which we now live, or simply pass the time, it is against the laws of nature to endure.

Here, even the most fundamental truth is condemned to being nothing more than a passing "wave." For example, even serious works on ecology (right along with the friendly, gushing alternative press) will soon be exiled from bookstore shelves to the special-interest corners, as were the tomes of scholarly leftist schools. Within the most minimal amount of time, the media get tired of all the croaking, the movement gets tired of itself before even the tiniest steps are taken toward improving the common weal. Weariness is the absolute sovereign of our culture. If there should ever be a so-called catastrophe, it will probably take place at a time when we just aren't interested anymore, and we will allow ourselves the luxury of a yawning shock.

Paradoxically, just this moment would be the poet's hour, at the highpoint of irrelevance in his existence. At this point, nothing could be more exemplary and useful than a talent for breaking with *his time*, bursting apart the chains of the present.

But in this society, aren't we merely one minority among others, one group of cripples among others, who long ago gave up our claims to the universal validity of our speech? Haven't the forces of diversity, the grand scrolls of a thousand fads and correctnesses made us incapable of taking an eccentric or avant-garde stance, opposite that of an albeit imaginary *whole*, thus giving it shape? I am not talking about the journalists who call themselves writers, and always know how to address the issues of "our times." I am only talking about the difficult players, the heirs to the modernists, the uneasy traditionalists, the pompous mannerists, and all the others who in the eyes of the majority are nothing but useless crackpots. And of those there are only a few, a dwindling few. And now, of all times, where consumption has become total (and here, what the fringe groups are reading is no different from what the book-of-the-month club serves up), there is no new literature, which, in rejecting this consumerism, might gain considerable strength, and bring about a current that would not itself turn into a celebration of being late, being based on nothing but French dregs and Artaud's anemic whispers. But in a time when literature itself has become an outsider in our culture, the outsider *in* literature has been forced out of his eccentric role. The official business of fashions and trends has taken the place of the new, i.e., the latest news is now the new. And in general, the critical mind seems to be having an allergic reaction to the new in its broadest sense; in keeping with the times, it is just now learning to make more intensive use of what we already have. But an avant-garde that is not convinced that the general public, the mediocre retinue, will one day take over their positions and elevate them to the status of common property lacks the fighting energy needed for its task. But who could now be so blind to his calling, and believe in the indisputable destiny of literature in the same way, say, a Mallarmé did, being convinced that the work of the world would be fulfilled in The Book. Today, to elevate the book to the status of metaphor for the universal archive of our culture would be nothing but a private pleasure, as harmless as it was obsolete. Supposedly, the work of the mind will end in eighty-seven television channels, and Mallarmé's book will become the cult object of a tiny secret society at the University of Wisconsin, and only there and nowhere else in the world will its memory be honored. Where writing itself vanishes from the center of culture, the outsider among writers, the eccentric, will become a foolish figure – a radical reaching for roots on a continent that is simply slipping away.

. . .

I would hate to think that the only cause of Nietzsche's illness, which ended with a progressive softening of the brain, was a luetic infection. This has always sounded like the malicious mystification of a philistine imposed on Nietzsche, the evil man. Furnished with a sensitive soul, which led to revolutionary writings overwhelming the whole writer, which in turn led to a cruelly heightened loneliness, which in turn brought about an inner inhumanity and the roar of a man – roots will bind anyone this radical to themselves.

N's often delighted handshaking.

Softheadedly lovable; in need of protection. Safekeeping! Safekeeping . . . just so long as it's not too strenuous. His mother: "I put my right hand on his forehead and read to him, then he always kisses my hand and whispers: 'I adore you, my dear sweet mother!' "

I have never patted horses, N. often says, because he just can't bring himself to say "loved." In Naumburg he takes a bath in a puddle, strips naked. His mother can't find him anywhere. But here he comes walking along with a policeman.

. . .

These days, we almost always think of them as the great sufferers: Kleist, Hölderlin, Nietzsche, Kafka, Celan. They are the only authentic ones. The guarantors of our more modest fate of simple dismay. But how shall we take leave of our minor fate? Nothing is simpler, and more vain, than to plant in ourselves the seed of a scream once brought forth by another human being, shattering in his greatness.

. . .

We can also clone styles and gestures. We can strive to be like one person or another, but there is really nothing to be gained. Literary passion quickly becomes a device: a vending machine of gestures. Goethe's gesture has been wandering through German poets for more than a hundred years. Today, Hölderlin's gesture and Artaud's provide us protection. That is to say: *we* outsiders, *we* unprotected – you, Hölderlin, and I who recognize you. There is a form of veneration that has lost all reserve in regard to unrelated greatness. At those times, the desire to borrow some kind of heroicism for our own unseemly pain gets the upper hand with us good citizens.

. . .

"The poet," Valéry says, "produces what he is driven to produce. Using his own inner resources, he constructs pseudo-mechanisms which are capable of giving him back the energy it cost to produce, and even more." Why should any man have any other reason for beginning a work of art, except the expectation that in succeeding it will enhance his life energies. This theory is a little more Roman and a little more given to the joys of life than those of flaws, sublimation, subjective pain, or social duty. There is always joy in this More of energy that a work of art contributes to the aggregate pleasure in the world, be it only a minute quantity. There is always joy, artistic, in a disintegrated novel, a painfully interrupted verse, a ringing labyrinth, a Tachist sign. Even joy in the bloody excrement we sweep in the direction of the lamia. There is no art of nondelight.

. . .

A "pre-aesthetic *parti pris* for material and information," is how Adorno described Lukács's literary theories, and it still determines the bald-faced interest of the masses in a work of art. Yet, you have to be a little shocked when it turns up as the ruling criterion in a young, curious public, as soon as a book or a film is to be examined. *Is it really necessary to repeat what has already been said?* Apparently, the great aesthetic teachers of our generation have had little or no impact on the present. With the exception of a few of the better feuilletons, nothing is being handed down. The interest of young people, as lively as it is, remains largely unencouraged.

No longer dependent on any intellectual authority, or admonished into silence, so that certain horizons, as was the case with us back then, simply will not be allowed to be overshadowed, now opinion is being led by a rather more sickly, egocentric naïveté with a wealth of rundown terms. Naturally, in intellectual life there is no place for a belief in linear progress. Positions and insights that had once penetrated a relatively broad spectrum of consciousness now can and must be ignored for some period of time. But the bad habit of evaluating a work of art solely on the basis of its critical utility, to measure it either on the basis of subjective "impact," or monotonous social criticism, tends to undermine the freely symbolic order of art. But, when profits and messages come first, and the delight in play with aesthetic signs and reflections, even the delight in beauty, threaten to rot, the productive mind, which art can provide every one of us, does not continue to develop, but becomes so diminished that it can be exchanged without hesitation for the passive archive of the TV-man.

. . .

The bus driver who has deposited a load of theater fans at the circus tent in which a contemporary play with a social conscience is being performed, and who then joins the audience, but only for a while, before leaving the tent without a word, upset, goes back to his empty bus, sits down behind the wheel, then drives off furiously and aimlessly through the streets. Why? Because in this play, from the very beginning, "the same old middle-class shit" was the target of scorn, because *his* homelife, *his* environment, his clothing, his opinions, and his family were being exposed to ridicule, because he himself was obviously insulted.

If the public is no longer willing and able to understand the symbolic language of a play, when it can only relate the place and substance of a play directly to its own sphere of experience, its own reality, on a 1:1 basis, why shouldn't there be this kind of revolt, though in fear of losing its identity to the theater, of the naive and the wild in art? At one time works of art protected us from the total dictatorship of the present.

The nineteenth-century group of painters who called themselves the German-Romans, foremost among them Feuerbach, turned away from the "*Sauepoche*" of early industrialism, and the "ideals of Humanism," and to the examples set by classical Italian painting. In the meantime, we no longer have any reason to disparage their stance as arrogant escapism, or the ecstasy of restoration. For this to be true, progressivism in art would have to mean much more than it actually does. To what extent a work of art is in congruence with its era, exhibiting a proximity to the present, to what extent it can be credited with breaking new ground and making great leaps forward, not only in a technical and formal sense, has long since ceased to be the most exciting course of critical investigation. There are circumstances when a painter obviously "cannot paint but what he paints," even when this means a determined break with his own era, that he produces a more remarkable portfolio of the contemporary than others who, always chasing the breaking day, attempt in times of radical change to answer new with new. In this sense, when we view Feuerbach's great works today, we see less the monumentality of noble illusion; the obsession with ancient mannerism is more clearly understood as a radical vision of historical sanctuary; his regal figures as the paranoia of a virtuous similarity with man, elevated creatures of a powerful loss anxiety at the threshold to a world of wild transformation. Today, when we stand in front of the *Pieta* at the Schack Gallery in Munich, Feuerbach's anachronism has an unsettling effect. All the schoolbook fraud is out the window; we see the unity of outline and form. The iconography complete, quiet, sustained, outsized, the emotional bearing of old painting; at the same time, it makes careful use of a few details of sensual mass which are features of "modern" realism, albeit a realism with an idealistic bent, which saves representation from empty formulism, as well as the all too neighborly feelings of the viewer.

The figure of Mary Magdalene kneeling at the Corpus Christi, her face veiled, has thrown herself across his chest, wailing. Her left hand – a limp, crooked, enervated paw – is lying in the hollow of the right collarbone of the corpse, lying there as if on a platter, in such a way that the sensuality of the dead flesh being mourned could not possibly be more emphasized. A hand lying like this can only be lying across lifeless matter. We could say: this hand is resting on the Corpus like the hand of a cook who has fallen asleep on the bread board. The crown of thorns is lying next to the bedstead, next to the dangling arm of the Saviour, like a set of dentures that a drunk has torn out of his maw before going to sleep. Then suddenly, the viewer is overcome by the irresistible urge to make such rude comparisons, and he knows that somewhere, for one moment, for one street-scene long, the painter saw something in his everyday surroundings which possessed the lines and the forms of the *Pieta* (as has been documented in this case). And: the eyes of the forms imprinted themselves on the banal pretext and the form gained new life thanks to the banality of what was seen. Together, form and discovery make up the fist of a work, its thrust, its power to prevail. This is why, in the later painting, there is such a striking resemblance between our perceptions and the *Pieta*'s unattainable gesture of mourning. This gesture exists solely in the realm of (art) history, in, let us say, a time-space melding together Raphael's *Devotion* and Feuerbach's *Rail Journeys*. It could never actually appear, even in a perfectly staged, perfectly lighted scene with ideally proportioned human beings that we might photograph or film. It is the historicality *in* a great picture that we take in so appreciatively and which provides us deliverance, for a time – not from the worries of the everyday and reality, quite the contrary, they are with us looking on, but deliverance from the agonies of an illusionary optics which the totally chronological one-dimensionality of photographic prints has imposed on us. For this reason alone, we breathe deeply in front of a painting, because it is both image and anti-film-image, at the same time. Not the written word, not music, first and paradoxically it is painting which has been able to cleanse us of the visual garbage corrupting and burdening the senses. There is no better incineration aggregate than the imaginary illumination of a great picture.

• • •

Heidegger (in his book on Heraclitus): "All essence is in truth non-pictorial. It would be wrong to perceive this as a deficiency. When we do this we are forgetting that it is the non-pictorial, and thus the invisible, which provides everything pictorial its cause and necessity. Without the invisible, which makes visualization possible, everything visible is only an optical stimulation." (Why else would we be so weary of what is increasingly graphical, while at the same time so greatly lacking in *essence*, as in most of the newer films?)

. . .

Now, all I want to say is: "a house." I hate saying: "a timbered house," "a clinker," "a paint job that looks like it was done with sandpaper," etc. Every kind of classifying description contributes to the evil of distraction, which is already such a great menace. When we write, we are also taking action against the individual view, beating back the apt detail. We have lived too long on the wealth of differentiation. Everything interesting is gross, and the same; real is less.

. . .

Rustling of causes: we do something, take off our clothes at night, take the lid off a pot, or drop a cap, then it stirs, suddenly in the sounds, and we let our minds wander off somewhere far away. I yearn for the shouts in the desert, the way I heard them from Sarah and Yukel in Edmond Jabés's books. A dialogue, shouted, with lots of echo, a most delicate exaltation, one over the other. A speaking that is itself the most perfect act of self-consumption, a smart – an unfulfilled love.

Absolute leisure, *free* time, does not really exist until waiting has vanished completely.

Ernst Jünger on continuous reading: "If every day you stack up a few more bricks, in sixty or eighty years you can be living in a palace." Can this really be true? In the end, might not the wise old man be sitting in front of an open, burned-out house with a door hanging loosely from one hinge?

. . .

Home comes to mind (though it was no refuge) when I read *Minima Moralia* again. How conscientious and splendid our thinking was back in those days! It seems that any number of generations have passed since then.

(Without dialectic we suddenly think dumber; but that's the way it has to be: without it!)

Instead, we are accompanied by a few younger thinker-satirists, the ethno- and anarcho-essayists, and we have no choice but to accept their brash assertiveness, these giggling violations of form aimed at the rigidly dogmatic Marxists and the orthodoxies of the academic world, in which they were so doggedly anti-everything that their own fantasies could hardly have taken wing. To waste so much energy confronting the kind of idiocy that defeats itself is not an indication of a strong desire to learn. We will not become elegant fencers practicing on scarecrows. But these are clever heads, and for the most part critics; no plans, nothing inventive, nothing liberating or dismaying can be expected from these quarters. And as long as no one greater has a say, we will continue to be entertained by their impudent hodgepodge.

"He writes well, the satirist, clever and to the point!" (Yes, he certainly does. The more clever his wit, the more ill-considered.) "Delightful!" (Yes, it certainly is delightful to the haggard. Caustic reason is dumb. Even your point of view has become superfluous. The first to be injured by a cutting wit is the wit himself.)

"And it is no less important to understand us dark, limited and dull souls, than is the understanding of the enlightened, the sensitive and the witty." (Gombrowicz, *Ferdydurke*)

Foucault: "In the final analysis, thinking must be this: very intense, from very close up, almost losing yourself while observing stupidity; weariness, inertia, a great tiredness, a determined muteness, and indolence form the flip side of thinking – or rather its accompaniment, its daily thankless occupation, which prepares it, and it then supplants."

How little we really care any longer about an all too middling intelligence; while caring all the more about a discerning dopiness.

Melancholy thought, or calm and composed, Kierkegaard, Heidegger, Lévi-Strauss. The anti-impertinent, if it is still possible to be using the term *anti* after these last one hundred youthful years, after the "Anti"-age of Nietzsche.

For Flaubert, simply living-from-day-to-day was too strenuous. His friends report that in the middle of the day he was often overcome by apathy and obsessive sleepiness. Sartre calls it his "pompous laziness." However, for every artist, and especially storytellers, going dark is an indispensable means of perceiving, and at the same time a defense against the piercingly concrete of his all too immediate surroundings. Concentrating, being transfixed, on the one hand; being impassive to the point of going gaga and losing oneself, on the other. (Even Benn mentions the morbid sleepiness he suffered on social occasions.) Before geese can leave the ground, they must get themselves into the appropriate mood for flight. A poet gets into the mood for flight through stupidity and indolence.

. . .

We don't know how dumb we are; or what unspeakable things we do. Every written work which an author completes shows him that (during the time he was writing) he was in command of an unimagined naïveté. No matter how carefully and thoroughly a text has been worked out, the form that allows for a conclusion douses the whole with an adventurous innocence. How could I ever have written anything like that? The end of a work is the one single moment when inspiration touches the author.

. . .

Referring to an author about whom a critic has not got one good word to say, he concludes with the observation: "But his greatest weakness is: he has absolutely no sense of irony about himself." Still, it seems to us, an author would be doubly contemptible if he couldn't even take his own obvious weaknesses seriously.

. . .

Duty paid by the intelligence of the mind (criticism) to the intelligence of sensuality. Hitchcock's *The Birds* will stay with us longer than Brecht's *Mother Courage*. One of these belongs to our mythology, the other to our studies. *Doxa* leaves and the rest of us stay behind in a thicket of excitation.

. . .

Absolutely nothing is grounded. Decay rules in the earth, the all-consuming primary image (the pure symbol, the "birds"). Everything grounded, learned, intelligently civilized, is like an ungainly pedestal about to close itself off. There will be no more relieved figures emerging out of this base.

. . .

Not "two cultures" but the pool, the consumption culture's entirety of today in the head of a human being; contributions from Ernst

Jünger and The Clash, from the fantasy novel and the RAF, from Black Botin and the Ozu-Retrospective; contributions that overlap one another, split and criss-cross. A memory full of outlines, fragments, temperaments, missing pieces, ignorance, and the medial pretense of totality. This is how it looks "on the frontiers of the archaic period of upcoming art," of a phase of renewal that will be characterized by the displacement of the predominance of the written word as well as the loss of a figurative realism, a phase in which forms of rational thinking are preparing for "a return to a diffuse and multi-dimensional thinking." And *Gesture and Speech*, the great work by Leroi-Gourhan on the "evolution of technology, language, and art," on the unlocking of the human mind, reads like one of the last books that once more sums up and thinks out ahead on the subject of the elementary conditions of the phenomenon homo sapiens in natural history, perhaps in order to pass it on to a totally transformed fellow being of the near future.

. . .

Wanting to escape the nightmares of the everyday, and finding no sustenance in the shredded forms of contemporary poetry, while, however, doing so in Rilke's *Elegies*, we are always trying to convince ourselves that hymnic beauty, if only deep enough, emerges out of the most parched soil, and is always the highest goal of poetry, a beauty discerning junk.

. . .

These days, literature hardly needs the forces of chaos. Certain shockwaves and currents of a subversive *fantastique*, still, but then: human intelligence would have to takes its place.

. . .

Love for literature, once as expansive as the universe, now in an infinitely slow retreat, possibly ending in the mass-concentrate of the few sayings of Heracles.

. . .

The loneliness of writing is probably even greater for contemporary authors than it was for those in the past who garnered little recognition during their lifetimes. While now they are all spoiled by the day, they have been cheated of any hope for posterity.

. . .

The Arnulf Rainer exhibit. How art has become diminished in the extremes of self-representation. The *I*-ness of the last two decades, namely the frantically heightened variant in Austrian art, is aimed at getting every last bit (socially ostracized, philosophically insignificant, enduring only in the figure of the artist himself) of whatever is to be had out of the individual, even at times endowing it with a religious ardor. Still, from one day to the next, this art shifts into another era of perception, suddenly giving the impression of having completely run its course and ended up a little disappointing. Part of the reason for this might be that this *I*-ness, while suffering, screaming, etc., has always been extraordinarily convinced of itself, its position, its hour, its mission. That in his works the absence of the *other* (whether faces, or story) very seldom is sensed as a great loss for art. As long as the monomaniacal manner still demanded that it be the focus of our entire attention, the limitations, for which it had itself to thank, were of little consequence. But now we take another look and perceive the limitations more clearly, and sense the inherent strength of the work beginning to diminish. In time, it is as if the style, which had defined the attempt, gradually emerged as the most lasting aspect of the work, while, on the whole, the effect of what was created and made manifest was not nearly as strong. Even in Rainer's death portraits (and painted death masks), the question arises as to whether or not the effect of the object itself is not too compelling. Of course, the subject chosen did elevate the tone of the gesture, and the artist certainly succeeded in nothing less than painting the return of the living in these death masks. Yet, it still seems to me that what the catalog of the exhibit refers to as the "singular impact" has been too easily ensnared. (In the meantime, it is possible that we have come to expect that anything really distressing will only emerge from what is inconspicuous and coincidental.) This will be the era of the gesture, the precise and fleeting movement, that will be preserved in this art.

What these works all lack is the space in which their battle for creation takes place; not one of these pictures exhibits any sense of having struggled for its essence. On the level of an art of existential radicalism, which runs through all currents and branches of modernism and post-modernism, and to which Rainer's work also belongs, this art suddenly seems to us poorer by that banal dimension that sets the created above a merely reflected physical reality. In this sense, in Francis Bacon's pictures the creation of space, the positioning of the cage, and the capturing of time are powerful acts of conception, without which the face caught up in the fullness of its movements would never appear, without which these bodies formed of contortion, of life and death muscles, would never emerge the way Jacob does out of his struggle with the angel.

dimmer

I must have been running, even racing, if not charging along that hot country road, because the animals of the field – the partridge, the hare, the lizard, the shrew – froze, as if lamed by a compression wave they had never sensed before, one that preceded my motion, and only after an unusually protracted paralysis did they flit or jump away. I came to myself again in a mountain village punctuated by antique ruins, looking as if it might have been patterned after an imaginary tableau out of the seventeenth century. As they sluggishly made their way up the slope, I followed a few naked men whose backs were flecked with small, curly clumps of hair. Some of them turned around and I looked into their faces, and they were idiots, feebleminded. I slowed my pace and stayed a short distance behind them. On the crest of the hill, there was an old fortress lying in ruin. I was told that there was a swimming pool for elephants on the inside. The idiots took me into their group as we approached a high, rusty, iron door. We opened the door a crack, and, truly, there was a splendid horde of bright gray elephants dancing with ponderous grace around their own axes, every large banner of an ear waving, and the motion of the heavy weight of their bodies bobbing up and down so delightedly made me feel as though I were watching them in natural slow motion.

We stood on the uppermost landing of a stone stairway. And I watched the face of a diving elephant in the pool. When this one finally climbs out, I thought to myself, we will find ourselves cowering before a colossus that at the moment can only be vaguely perceived in its squat, distorted form, under the trembling surface of the water.

At this very same moment, I clumsily shoved open the iron portal through whose half opening we had first looked in, and I slammed a sharp, rusty edge against the trunk of an elephant that was standing behind it. It fell over, and a bloody gash, the kind humans get on the bridge of the nose when it gets squeezed by a pair of tight-fitting glasses, opened up on its trunk. It looked at me out of one eye, infinitely sad. Not angry. I ran to one of the keepers who were hanging around outside the swimming area or lying on the ground. I had a leaden, profoundly grieving conscience and was afraid of having injured the elephant more seriously than was at first apparent. I was also reluctant to bring this mishap, which was after all my fault, to the attention of one of these keepers. But I had to do it. However, the man to whom I reported the overturned creature did not lift a finger; he was totally indifferent and said everything would take care of itself. I did not go back to the gate, and was so ashamed, that here in the realm of weight and beauty, which I was allowed to enter in the retinue of the feebleminded, I was the first to show my clumsiness by knocking over a gentle elephant, not having managed to simply stand by and watch passively, like all the other debilitated.

. . .

As I continued on my way, I came across a chorus on the side of the road. It was a monkly dark, Barlach-like, bronze sculpture of men wearing caps, figures melded into one another, each growing out of the one preceding, under the strain of unknown troubles, a standing, half-round, constant sorrow, empty eye sockets and round Oh!-holes instead of mouths, masks behind which there should be actors. This was an indication that at some time we would each have to step behind them. The structure of doubt and melding stands empty and ready. Before us was a work frozen in throbbing fright. Somewhat smaller than lifesize. A half-round, arched outward.

. . .

I came to a road and could not see that it was built in the form of a ribbon, the form of the intertwining zeroes of the infinity sign. There, just left by two mechanics, was a Saab, waiting for me with an open door and registration papers tucked under the windshield wipers. A young woman, a child, was sitting on her suitcase next to the car. I asked what she wanted. To go to Brussels, is what the young woman who got into my car wanted. Dawn breaking in a stony gray sky. We did not speak. Withdrawn, she looked off to the side, rested her chin on her knee. Pearls of sweat, of the most solitary being-left-to-oneself. Then she began to content herself by taking my sex into her mouth. I understood that we were gliding into a world of absolute sexual indifference. Humans closed off, profoundly lost in thought, in their entire beings somewhere very far away, diving calmly and weightlessly on the surface of what is human, when a pornographic chimera tempts, they surface, only to render an imaginary image, an engaging play of figures, and then they dive again. Without harm and without hope. Their visit to the realm of man is a visit to the wonderland of obscenity.

Naked chick! I pushed her breastless torso between my legs, pressed the palms of both hands into her small, damp armpits, and stared at her narrow, chafed baby ass.

Human sexuality and its culture were once the reservoir of myth – the silent realm of the gods, of these mysterious beings who disappeared into the underworld. From time to time, a tired need to love while remaining tired, brought them up to us.

. . .

My trip was like a tour of a movie lot, where, of course, no work was being done, but the spirits of scenes and motives long ago shot provided the backdrop for a gloomy rendezvous. Behind the facade of a rest stop the only guestroom was already taken: father mother daughter son locked together on a soiled mattress, like the ones found in refugee camps, the little family. Like this, in one of Blake's drawings, lying next to one another on a bier: the chancellor, the king, the warrior, mother and child. The warrior, legs crossed, hand on the hilt of his sword, was resting in the middle. Here, the two old people were sullenly clinging to one another, fear and red and blue spots on their faces. The daughter, her hair tied back, rises in her sleep and gently pulls up her nightgown. She kneels straight up over her brother. She grasps his outstretched sex and inserts it, like a bar of soap, into her vagina. Admonitions begin coming from the parents, urgent pleas, to have pity and leave it be. The daughter climbs down off the man, and asks how he would like to have her. Disinterestedly, the brother says: "Turn around!" So, she turns her ass to him and stares, in closest proximity, while now both moan, openly, absently, into the faces of the two old people who are embracing each other even more tightly. They protest more and more strongly and scream: "Stop! Come on, just stop this!" Yes, I thought, that is the memory, that's it: everything incest. The cities, the hours, the steps down, down . . .

. . .

The guard and the most dangerous prisoner of all time (even in the Disneyland of loneliness, we can't get along without superlatives) are jailed together in a cramped, steel cage fixed on the top level of a raised concrete track – a straight and empty track, stretching endlessly north and south so that no one has any idea what structure it belongs to, or in what realm it might belong. The two-man cage sits alone on a wide, very wide corridor, and it seems as if the molecule of all captivity had been isolated and exposed. Above, on his level, even with the concrete track, the guard is sitting on an unusual, high-backed chair, on a ridiculous throne, we might say, while the prisoner is lying or lounging around at his feet, on the floor, without seating, only in flat, buttoned-up clothing, but free to move, without chains or handcuffs. His gun on his knee, the guard bends over stiffly and looks down through thick glasses at his – no: at the prisoner, because the grated ceiling laced with barbed wire and broken pieces of glass hangs so low over his head that he can never really straighten up without injuring the skin on his head. From the side, two neon tubes provide light. In addition, a searchlight, whose location is impossible to determine, shines across the cage at irregular intervals. But all the guard does is sit, he is belted in so that he won't, should sleepiness overcome him, sink down to the level of the one who is to be watched. At this point, we are no longer talking about: the prisoner. We are not talking about: the guard and his prisoner. We are not even talking about: the guard and the prisoner. Now, we say: the watcher and the one to be watched, because here in the most cramped of compartments, in the proto-cell of world prison, so to speak, we stumble onto a kernel of mutual devotion, a silent up and down of punishing and enduring is the plasma, no matter that one must stay up on top while the other stays down below. And yet, when one of them speaks, the watcher is always first and he often spits out brusque orders down toward the floor: "Move it. Don't just sit there. Do something. Hands in your pockets. Wave. Clap. Shadowbox. Sit up straight. Listen. Hand up to your ear. Not up here, up is not your direction. Damn it all, of all people, why me, how did I ever end up being your guard!? Make something up for me." As always, the one who is to be watched quickly assumes the role of the naked watcher, who, like a chimpanzee, is hanging from the bars outside the cage, wanting badly to get back to the place he was directed to stay, and in so doing he gashes himself open on the broken pieces of glass. The guard mumbles wearily: "I am not allowed to raise my head, I have to keep looking down at you. You aren't allowed to look up, because that would be an uprising."

. . .

Emptiness. Repetition. The absolute is the allowing of the everyday to ring. Life takes place in the hallway. Four boys are walking through, speaking quietly, keeping silent most of the time. "Do you know the Metaland disco?" – "Yes, sure." Speaking without enthusiasm, without urgency. That's how everything is. It's like that. Rockhardness of the hall monitor. Foamy thread from which your life is hanging, your own spittle on which you are swinging through the air like a little spider.

. . .

Proto-form of the meaningless, the insignificant, and the leap of *sweet happening* – as inseparable as the head and the tail of a coin.

. . .

For a little while, from your hiding place, keep throwing pebbles at the pianist singing to himself, and then steal out of this languorous garden forever. As if it were possible to tolerate any society, no matter what sort!

. . .

Animals, plants, gods and thinking – none of them is a friend of man. Having come to the point of looking, at the very height of instruction. For us, one single word seeing beyond the mountain would suffice.

. . .

One single rider on the train of beginning, racing through the night brightly lit, is Mr. End, dark passenger.

So much forgiving in death! – how much longer now? So much deferral. A dense jungle of signs full of his revelations and omens, this is our entire route.

. . .

Whenever I cross the corridor, said a man whose reincarnations had always forced him back into the same office, and the same bureaucratic existence, whenever I go from my office into my director's, I see a female person leaning out the window at the end of the corridor. I have never not seen her. And looking at it from my doorway, the corridor is not a short one. I would have to walk for a long time, for a very long time, before getting to this person. Well, there is always a woman leaning out the window, the director says, and smiles contentedly, when once in a relaxed moment I ask him about it. But just imagine: it is a wax figure. The rear part, which you see, does not belong to a living being. Seen from the street, this figure embodies an alluring idleness, which makes our office look quite congenial in the eyes of passersby. And we – we go about our work behind this sweet symbol, this wax statue of everlasting indolence. This is how I explained it to myself, and since that time I have always wanted it to be this way.

. . .

That man over there is not interested in anything anymore. Still some effort, to keep himself stumbling around a bit. Or sweeping up the sand in front of the house. And it's good like this. Good. And a little rest in front of his house after he's done. He'll survive, this man of the infinitely drawn out "Yes!" He's still holding onto something, but just one thing.

That unrecognized woman with the short black hair, who for the span of an average man's life has been walking out in front of him, and while pushing her sunglasses down on her nose, her little nose, always turned around and looked at him mockingly to see if he were still following her, and he couldn't help himself, he had to keep following, forever, godknowswhere. He had never seen her from the front. But this time, in front of his house, he was first. He had actually passed her. At any moment now she will be coming around the corner, he thought, and it won't be long before I will have looked into her face. And that is how it happened.

. . .

One of today's rulers appeared, only to toss a smoldering cigarette butt out of the window in such a way that it fell in a high arc out onto the square where some of his subjects were idly waiting and looking up into the brightly lit windows of the conference room. The cold blade of the constitution raced over the highly arched napes of their democratic necks.

. . .

The cabin of an ocean giant pitched and rolled on an artificial piece of sea, where turbines simulated the raging wind and waves. Inside, where all the dishes are threatening to fall out of the open and listing cupboard, the young daughter of the chief steward is trying to keep them on their shelves. The rib of the ship rolls port-side, and with hands spread wide, stretched high on the tips of her toes, the little one is leaping back and forth across the front of the cupboard, pushing back a cup here, there a sliding plate just about to plunge. Despite the churning waters, her father, the chief steward, is managing to keep his hands in his pockets and stand straight and threatening in the background. He watches the desperate exertions of the child. Each time there is one more dish about to fall, he yells brusquely: "Kein Fahrrad." Or, at another moment, harsh and curt: "Niemals glücklich." Which basically means: if it falls, you won't get a bicycle, you will never be happy, etc. The falling piece *is* a bicycle never to be received. But while I too am doing no more than standing next to the chief steward, making no attempt at all to help the child do her damned work, a sentence of Auden's, which I recently read in Julien Green's journal, keeps churning around in my head: "The crack in the teacup is the path which leads us into the land of the dead!" and I am nauseated from anxiety and dizziness. But then, all of a sudden, it is me to whom the father entrusts his little daughter, entreating me to take her on shore, to a hotel, and put her to bed. It is the shock of the lamia I always suffer when my prey is laid trustingly into my arms, as if someone were intent upon nothing else but rousing my basest instincts and brutally coaxing the destroyer of children to come out. I also know that at these times I have always been enveloped with the poisonous aura of good nature and selflessness that invariably wafts out in front of all evil.

. . .

Looking for her room in the tangle of the hotel's corridors, the young woman comes upon a man in a white shirt and black trousers, standing in the shadows of a narrow, dimly-lit hallway. He is resting the backs of his hands against his hips, and there are three plates in his hands. From time to time, he holds the hands with the plates out in front of him, looks at them, as if the hands with the plates did not belong to him, turns them over and again rests the backs of his hands against his hips. Maybe he juggles plates, but he has no pole. Maybe he is simply a man who has never had to hold three plates in one hand before. In any case, he does not have the slightest idea what to do with the plates, out here in the corridor, doors closed left and right. He seems not to know how the plates ended up in his hands, or even how he himself came to the corridor with the plates in his hands, nor what he should now do. Without losing its glow, the bulb hanging from the ceiling falls to the floor and smashes, forming a light puddle and suddenly illuminating the man with footlights from below.

The daughter of the chief steward smiles at this incident, and believes we have now seen how someone might not have any option but to become an artist.

. . .

Once she is lying in bed and looking at me with big open eyes, I try, without her having asked, to tell her a bedtime story to help her get to sleep and me to stay calm.

So, what would you like to hear, you enlightened creature? A true story is what I would like to tell you, before your clever head sinks down into the pillow. Would you like to hear "Men and Women" or "A Letter is Missing from the Alphabet"? "A Letter is Missing from the Alphabet" is a story about how the twenty-seventh letter was stolen, and how the white space between words came to be, and how the whole language had to be redone, from the beginning, once the twenty-seventh letter was finally found again. Well, okay, you'd rather hear "Men and Women." Fine.

In the beginning, the two sexes were not created for one another. Men and women lived as good neighbors in peace-loving tribes, and they traded their wares with one another. Each of the sexes had splendid and useful goods the other needed. The women, for example, possessed pasture land, cinemas, and sandwiches, while the men had hydrochloric acid, diamonds, and flour to trade. At this time, there was still no love and no hate among humans. What everyone loved most were the things they made and used for exchange. They loved only their own things. Back then, even death was a good friend of mankind, and it was fruitful. Birth and death were one, and death gave life. Every time a man lay down to die a boy crawled out of his body, and every time a woman lay down to die a girl crawled out of hers. This life, in which the only difference was between work and idleness, and the difference between man and woman was no more important than the difference between two other ordinary things, like stone and grass, or hopping and waving, or cloth and salt, this life, which was neither happy nor unhappy, lasted for an undetermined period of time. Then one day, Mara, the princess and head worker of the women, lay down to die and bore an heiress to the throne. However, Mara remained only one day in the realm of the dead, and returned the next to take up her work again, thus shocking everyone, but she was a very trade-obsessed woman.

This angered the spirit of death, and from then on he denied all dying women fertility. Not one more girl came into this world. Greatly alarmed, the women prepared birthdeath god one opulent sacrificial festival after the other, though it was futile. They exhausted themselves and their resources to such an extent, becoming poorer and poorer, that they were soon in debt to the men, who for their part were becoming richer and richer. And this is how the inequality of the sexes came about, and half of creation appeared to be in danger of dying out.

At this point, the god of birthdeath saw that he could no longer play the role of the injured party, and he took out the slate he used to work out his plans and his logic for humankind, and he feverishly made his calculations to correct the imbalance. But in the end, he was not able to find the old equation of the sexes.

Desperate with himself, he threw the slate down on the ground, gave up the whole exercise and turned to other endeavors. This is how humankind came into possession of the shattered slate, this perplexing divine matter, and did not understand what was happening to them: everything gave way to chaos. The men died at the height of their powers and left behind two nuts. The women greedily ate up everything they had produced for trade and their own everyday needs. Everyone was running around aimlessly. Then one day, a few men and women suddenly greeted each other in utmost fear of perishing, and embraced each other. Then the women saw that the men made them fruitful, and they could give birth without having to die at the same time. But the men had lost their fertility forever, and they needed the women, who could now bring both girls and boys into the world, but only when men held them close. This is how, out of the discarded laws and the shards of divine wisdom, the unequal exchange between semen and children came to be, and love emerged as the sister of the formless horror a morose god, unable to find his old equation, brought down on humankind. The women were honorable, and loved and allocated the children fairly, the boys to the men, and the girls to themselves. However, the men, having become greedy, cheated the women, who now had to bear children several times over the course of their lives and could no longer adequately take care of their property. That is why, up to this very day, women have not forgotten what it was like before love, when they possessed half of all things.

. . .

At this moment, I became aware of the fact that all this time I had been standing on a high ladder, as high as a house, and made of wood, and next to me were hundreds of other spectators, standing at the same elevation in order to gaze over a white circular wall and watch a stage play none of us could ever have imagined in our wildest dreams. But a strong wind assaulted us head on, and lifted us, ladder and all, off the edge of the wall, threw us undulating into the air, and the ladders seemed about to tip over backwards. Many of us quickly climbed down several rungs in order to find our balance. But the wind, great breath that can even blow lazy rivers out of their beds, bent the ladders like a vaulter's pole, and those of us holding out on the upper rungs, hanging onto the play with every fiber of our being, were probably hoping to be lofted over the wall by the force of the recoiling wood, once the wind had died down. But we fell to the ground on our backs. A few of us lay crushed; others, though broken, crept away. There were roads through the fields and ancient, round gates made of rough-hewn stone blocks. . . . There is always a way, dusty, and an *old* exit leading out into the open.

by ourselves

At a Kanovitz exhibit, a number of visitors, each at his own pace, is quietly moving along from picture to picture. You think: this is a good place for you, alone among so many people by themselves, and doesn't an individual, now and then, still look as if he had been born to look? At the end, however, the loners clump together, and it turns out they all know each other, they belong together, they are a group that had only dispersed for the duration of the viewing. Even here you were far and wide the only one alone.

. . .

Lower District Court Tiergarten. Trial of the drug dealer, Ilona M., 29, on the needle since 1972, no vocational training, casual prostitution, violation of narcotics regulations, three arrests, now six months in Lehrte Women's Penitentiary, where she continues to shoot up and deal, appears now to be in "relatively good condition," according to the presiding judge, after she had met the defendant in private and taken her measure. Ilona is small, has reddish, dyed hair, a flat and very pale face, breasts and backside getting chubby, very slender torso; and the heavy, ample breastdrops do not seem to fit this body so wasted by heroin, such a motherly appeal in this lost child. Her voice, so very quiet and monotone that the prosecutor has to keep reminding her to speak more loudly so he can hear what he has already heard in a hundred similar cases, the drug addicts all lie, he knows that, they all tell the same lies and say they're ready to go into therapy for no other reason that to get probation. The judge says: "You really do speak very quietly. Is something wrong with your teeth?" Ilona: "I had them taken care of in the institution." But the defendant is not speaking quietly in order to appear especially helpless or to gain sympathy. While she testifies about her own person, and follows the sober, but not in the least harsh, tone of the inquiry, the reality of her situation is becoming clear to her: hopeless, she's becoming aware of what is otherwise obscured by the protective jargon of prison and the dope scene. The presiding judge has been working with drug addicts for more than twenty years, and is well known in these circles as "Mother Treats." Defense attorneys always consider it an advantage to have Mother Treats in charge of one of their trials. In this damned sphere, where the threat of punishment is of no use, if there is still anything at all to be done, it is possible that only the image of the kind, the kind and conscientiously admonishing mother can accomplish it. On the other hand, as a guardian of the law, she can hardly lead a fight against the illness of addiction; she has no other choice but to secretly give in to the total futility of the site and the proceeding at the center of which she herself is standing. Her rulings sound more like the most highly abstract form of offering help and protection to her problem *children*. Of course, she knows the dangers of probation, also knows where, how, and with what chances of success the last attempt at therapy can be undertaken, and basically her judicial task consists in challenging death sentences rendered long ago.

The prosecutor is a young, cold man whose role it is to play the part of the uncomprehending lout in these scenarios, and he is therefore nothing but an empty cliché of a prosecutor, no longer representing the state, which as everyone one knows has no particular interest in the prosecution of drug addicts anyway. In his brief, he goes so far as to maintain that the defendant is now in such an extreme state that she "can no longer be saved." Ilona's attorney is perfectly happy to hear this expression of unconcealed inhumanity, and he will make his case against this obvious malice.

But before that, there is a witness to be called. A young woman in a leather jacket, jeans, ankle boots, long wavy hair, amply doped, her eyelids keep drooping, her arms carry out strange, round, feeble motions. The judge explains very forcefully that the witness may refuse to answer any question which she believes may incriminate her. "Do you understand?" the judge asks once more, as if she were checking the witness's hearing. The young woman's voice is as quiet and monotone as the defendant's. At some point, however, her speech flips out, she circles around senselessly in the same few sentences. The prosecutor: "When was the last time you shot up?" The young woman came within a hair's breadth of answering: "Just now," but before this could happen, the judge swiftly intervened: "I have a suspicion that the witness is not presently fit to testify."

While the court retires for consultation, the young court stenographer, about the same age as the defendant and with similar clothing and hair, goes out into the hallway – at that moment, the bailiff, who had been reading *Kicker* magazine during the proceedings, leaps up from his chair, runs after her and attempts to haul her back in, having confused her with the defendant. While she has been talking with two friends who are sitting among the visitors, and have, on several occasions, mumbled complaints over the prosecutor's speech. Also sitting in the visitor's area are pupils from a school for social workers, along with their strict and dull-looking teachers. Ilona M. gets one and a half years without parole. Then, not without surprise, she hears that the court is revoking the current arrest order, and that because of this she will have one more chance, the last one, as Mother Treats underscores with bitter sorrow, to proceed immediately to a treatment center. It will be six weeks before she has to appear for sentencing. If, at that time, she is in therapy, her sentence will be commuted to parole. The presiding judge knows that jail will not help, and she says so in her arguments: there is no place where it is easier to get drugs than in the Lehrte Women's Prison. Even she must admit that in this case she herself does not hold out much hope. "Of course, you know," she adds, using an expression from stage German, "that once a drug addict is thirty years old, she is already a *well-developed character.*"

Once you have some sense of the horrible hopelessness and the threat to life that surrounds addicts, it becomes very difficult to take refuge in the search for social causes; unaccustomed, you stare at a naked, sovereign evil, the tangibly existent power of the devil. And it confronts us with one more mean grimace during a conversation with Ilona's friends following the end of the court session. The young man with scarred, ashen face, with large silkily shimmering eyes, arrested five times for drug crimes, and his girlfriend, attending the trial on leave from Lehrte Prison, say it's no good, really no good, Ilona has been released so suddenly, and out on her own recognizance. They are convinced that she'll be out looking for drugs by the time night falls. The woman says: "When you've been in Lehrte for so long, always all those restrictions, then you get out and you're in your own living room, and you don't know what to do any more, you don't even know where the telephone is." One of the treatment centers mentioned by the defense attorney, she says, is "a joke, justa joke." The woman: "The ones who go there all come back to Lehrte. Sure, everybody's happy to get out. I'd be happy, too, if I got out."

But, in truth, her words are an expression of the absolute opposite of concern for a friend. What we hear is the rage at having lost a business connection. In prison, Ilona ran an important branch of her drug operation. All senses a sense for business; no smile, no lie, no handshake, that wasn't a part of the addiction scene. Here, nothing is complicated or ambiguous any longer. Addiction is the one corridor into which all internal and external impulses flow. It does not seek some obscure happiness. The fulfillment of all wishes is manifest, and is, again and again, tediously and straightforwardly achieved. The tricks and the camouflage along the way, feigning friendly feelings, the delusions about your own situation are transparent in a way, as if they wanted to caricature this game with hidden intentions, in which we all participate in the most hideous possible manner. Although the addict shows us nothing but the raw stump of a free will, he is still in need of social finery. Things such as underground demeanor, the right addresses, secret contacts and meeting places, code-names and jargon (which the authorities now use without quotation marks) all belong to this cloak of quiet fanaticism without a message, often enough a deathly black, velvety soft cape enveloping these runaways with their pale faces, their pupils opened wide for nothing visible, with their rotting teeth and their thin sleep-inducing voices, which, when we hear them, make us ask: Who's that talking? *Who?*

A drug-dependent person is always enshrouded in a dense web of rhythms and rules, meetings and transactions, which he gives himself to without fantasy, without madness, without *weltschmerz*, because, as long as everything works out, he is, like no other, truly immune to the phantoms of the imaginary.

• • •

A drunk enters a dry-cleaning shop early in the morning. Maybe he has been drinking all night, but he is still speaking quite clearly, and he can stand up straight. Only his comprehension is gummy and his gaze is swimming. He shows a spot on his pant leg to the two women standing behind the counter. He would like to have it removed. The two women tell him that he will have to leave his pants there, it just isn't possible to remove a grease stain (was it? or only a hasty demure definition given to avoid closer inspection) in such a rush. After a short while, the man repeats his request using the same words over again; the two women explain one after the other, several times, that he will have to leave the pants there. They pay absolutely no attention to this man's special state of mind. But by treating the drunk like a sober man, or at most a hard-of-hearing man, while they neither show him out nor help him understand their explanation, they both appear to be especially rude, although it is actually embarrassment and apprehension that are causing them to behave so indecisively. For a moment, the drunk really does seem to be considering, very intently, very painstakingly, whether or not he should take off his pants. But since he is not a happy drunk but a dark and reserved one, a dull obstinacy in his soul keeps him from making himself into a clown in underpants in front of the women. For a short while he continues staring into this inalterable situation, then shrugs his shoulders and, sad-offended, leaves the shop. The women turn around and go into the back room to iron and mangle. With great zeal, they immediately go back to gossiping about a mutual friend, taking up where the drunk had just interrupted them. Sending not even a quiet shake of the head or a giggle in the direction of this curious man. Apart from exploitation and fear, the only other forces that seem to play a role in regulating the affairs of human beings among each other are negligence and indifference. And if you take away this profound indifference people have for one another, all you really do is increase their aggression.

. . .

The Mister Minit in a Munich department store, a slight, dark little man from the Rhineland, one who drifts around on the edges of society and who looks like those guys who used to run our scooter rides at the carnival, and who were always gruff with us because they really didn't have any feeling for children, and were never especially happy to see us having a good time, and in the eyes of children, a person who does not love children is asocial, a criminal, and most of them were released prisoners, just like this Mr. Minit here, who had probably learned the shoe repair trade behind bars. I ask him for a little name tag, just "temporary." "Hmm? Just temporary?" he asks, good-humoredly, "you keep movin' too?" Then an elderly man approaches the shoe stand. In a flash, the fraternal smile disappeared; suspicion and fright, sudden dulling in Mister Minit's eyes; instinctive fear of a beating. The man simply seems to be like one of those characters who were always his pursuers, who were always suspicious of him in one way or another. But perhaps he also looks like someone who had once fingered him, or maybe he even looked like a victim of the former criminal, Mr. Minit, himself. In any case, something brought him up short at the sight of this customer, and the man is served with extreme reserve, without a single amicable remark. Shortly thereafter, when a particularly well-dressed woman comes in and asks him to do a meticulous repair on her heels, everything is different; he becomes the eager professional again: "Very carefully, of course. Otherwise, they wouldn't have brought me all the way down here from northern Germany, I'm not some kind of know-nothing yokel." He had not only learned to combine an entrepreneurial zeal with an ability to ingratiate himself with his urban clientele, this thin-skinned outsider, this wanderer out of weakness was carrying around a cloak of clichéd behaviors, a coat of scales made up of formulas and adaptive pieces of attitude, and all his timorous talkativeness is nothing but a safeguard against suspicions that can be raised against people who are silent or just have a certain look about them. "I have to watch out for my good reputation," he adds, seeing no irony in what he has just said. A young shop apprentice walks by and shouts, wants to know if he needs another "empty pack." "Yes, all the time," the shoemaker shouts back, in a good mood, always a sense of masculine good spirits when someone makes reference to his vice, his true strength, drinking, that is. He smiles and talks to me like a buddy: "So, do you know whatta 'empty pack' is? A box with one last bottle of beer in it." Later, the chubby apprentice with a punk stud in his ear comes back and asks Mr. Minit, the undernourished drinker, if he will repair his boots. Sure, just bring 'em by, he answers, of course I'll do it. The young man: he'll have to wear a gas mask. The drinker: "I've got a spray, no problem. And, kid: when you pick up the boots and my colleague is here, tell him you paid already, it cost twenty marks." "Ya, got it." This is how the frail man made lightning-fast use of his outsider intelligence, let the apprentice know how much the work he was doing would have cost, twenty marks. Index for a corresponding number of "empty cases," or for other recompense. This all came about without a smile, or any hesitation – purely instinctive.

. . .

The man in the newspaper kiosk chides me because of the large number of overfilled shopping bags I am carrying. He quotes – he of all people, out from behind his ton of newspaper! – Diogenes, who once went to Corinth and then said: now I have seen all of the things I can do without.

. . .

Someone who is used to being on his own a lot, and making his own decisions, will always notice a gentle attenuation of his ability to observe when he finds himself in the shelter of a group, an advisory collective, or even one single other person. (Even traveling with one other person: All of the things you don't see, how diminished your attention!) You can only be in top form when you are alone, and you act unprotected, and every look is an act. Exposed from all sides, you must arm yourself with sharper perception, be quicker and more precise in the way you experience things than those who are allied, and are stronger. Your intelligence, neither extravagant nor superior, is closer to the animal instinct for survival than it is to the intelligence of a person assimilated into a group. By contrast, the character of a personality in charge, the authority, the leader, who needs, absolutely needs, the artificially diminished, downwardly rounded-off intelligence of the collective in order to energize himself and to prove himself to be the more intelligent being. The leader, who would be a perfect zero as a loner, who in an intimate dialogue so often appears to be a lackluster mediocrity of a soul, if not an idiot, not because it "doesn't really matter to him," but because his intelligence first begins to unfold at a certain temperature of superiority, that is, in the presence of no less than a dozen clustered, thus inferior, human beings. And even the most intimate impulses never come to him in silence, but only in those places where he exercises power. He only opens up out in the open.

. . .

You have often asked yourself what some people who distinguish themselves in the arts, who work with something so remote and so unliked by the public as today's art, what could possibly lead them to come out in public and to make themselves celebrities, right along with everyone's favorites in sports and show business; to become performers in an event of the highest level, but that is no longer really of any interest at all and will never be. And just as often, you have come to the conclusion that these people act purely out of a desire for recognition and not out of a sense of their intellectual mission, for no matter how outstanding this might be, any idea from any magazine off the rack would overwhelm it. (This medium is saturated through and through with the goal of entertainment. It is *always* cheerful, for as far as this medium is concerned, nothing really makes any difference.)

Therefore: never let yourself be caught by a flash, on film, in an interview, at an awards ceremony, and thankfully enjoy protection within the flow of the crowd. Against the backdrop of such convictions, you go to a museum, an exhibition of the century with a record number of visitors. Calm, collected, you cross the threshold and suddenly three men run up to you, flashes, spotlights glare, a woman with a microphone in her hand is standing in front of you. They have all been waiting for you; you are the hundred-thousandth visitor to the exhibit, and having crossed this threshold, you are now a public figure. You are given a picture book, and you cannot avoid taking a free tour of the exhibit conducted by the museum director, himself. And for days thereafter, your name is seen in the local paper, and a photo is printed, showing you as the museum visitor, chosen by the public, confused and thinking of taking flight, as you truly were. Nevertheless: no one identified you as the creator of art, prominent on the edge, the one who is from time to time discussed under other circumstances in the same newspapers. He remained unrecognized and undiscovered. Your real name has been used, but your profession has been given as "househusband." To that extent, it was awful and then it was okay.

. . .

The lonesome Punch of a figure who can hardly stand the outward appearance of himself sitting alone at a restaurant table gets up busily and stiffly several times and goes to the buffet, and sets the telephone receiver right, and then finally dials his own number at home, which causes the phone to ring in his own empty quarters and thus, receiver in hand and a look of solemn expectation on his face, he feels armed and occupied enough to gaze around at the people sitting in couples in the restaurant and seeming to him to be staring him down, who then, after a few minutes, with a feigned sigh of disappointment hangs up and goes back to his table.

. . .

Visit by a man from Kassel, who talked a lot and crazily, in order to say only one thing: "If you don't put me, fully developed artist and political man that I am, immediately in contact with a theater – and I only want the best! – then I will, I will have to release the bacillus of violence that is in me and run down into the ever narrowing refuge of the corridor of terrorism, down to its very end, where we will all be blown up . . ."

He kept talking about '68, about politicizing. "Then everything was politicized," he said, and then there came a resigned gesture of the hand, the way older people used to say: Then inflation came, then the war, then expulsion . . .

He wouldn't let go of his primal wound – once so sheltered, so unspeakably expelled, orphaned still, though today with his almost forty years. A crazy with sharp sight, but only for *his own* misfortune, and with the unmistakable threat that he will take it with him into the struggle against the state. "This is my last try. Keep me from taking up the career of an assassin! Find me a way into the theater!" As I said, we are dealing with a crazy. But can you help a man onto the stage who implores: For the sake of our dear peace, do not let me become a revolutionary!?

. . .

A memory for the year '78: In a restaurant in Düsseldorf's Old Town, they shot a young terrorist who had already gotten away from them twice. According to the news, a customer recognized him, of course they are as prominent as Wim Thoelke, and then called the police. When an officer dressed in street clothes approached his table, the terrorist allegedly drew his gun. He was beaten to his first shot by the many shots coming from the weapons of the authorities. It is difficult to escape the impression that in this way the intricacies of litigation might be avoided, since this has become a particularly sensitive weak point for the state. As long as he is in detention, it is possible that a terrorist may be "sprung," legally. "Kill immediately" seems to be the possibly secret, possibly express doctrine of all organs of executive power. Only a dead terrorist is a complete success, and a relief to us all.

The fact remains: a man who was suspected of murder has been shot – *if* he was the one whom an eager television viewer believed he had recognized in the thicket of immediate reality. Less still: a man who made the gesture of drawing a gun was immediately shot full of holes, even before he had threatened anyone with his weapon. But did he draw a weapon? This man's mind is playing tricks: you are quickly made a suspect, you are denounced quickly, you make a false move quickly. All of a sudden, two men are standing next to you and one of them asks for a light. You reach for your

idiots of the immediate

What is *anxiety*, what has become of it?

Two intellectuals: a couple about to find each other again, to renew the old, interrupted connection. She talks about how difficult for her the relationship with Heiner is; he thinks it's now finally time they take the trip they had once planned to take to East Germany, "if you'd really like to." For a while, with "flying baggage," the two of them are underway to new shores. But then, in the same conversation, the eagerness fades, things start going downhill, and they land at what they call "the very old, basic discussion between us." In this discussion, the man keeps using the expression: "I am terribly afraid, I really am," and he uses it so often that we might be led to believe that he's using this cliché to grease the machinery of his speech, the way other people do with a "if you'd like," or "I'll say." But what can this intellectual, already into his middle years, be so terribly afraid of?

He was terribly afraid of making a mistake in his relationship. But is that something that really deserves to be called fear? Can't this clump of nightmare, "relationship," always be diluted into babble, dissolved in the technical language of interchangeable parts we have learned to use to talk about the soul? Can't we express this a couple of sizes smaller, what this well-educated mind, carefully double-stitched, is referring to as his "terrible fear"? But our lives are filled with the kind exaggerations and emotional words we find in advertising: "Well, I'm awfully shocked by the fur collar on his overcoat." An extravagant, inflationary use of clichés of pain, a kind of hypochondriacal display being run by advertising for the sake of its own heightened sensibilities: shocked, moved, touched; all false, quivering tones of a subject whose heart is no longer capable of being astonished.

What will they say when one day they are confronted with extraordinary terror?

In our culture, where will we go to survive our anxieties?

To haunted dreams, of course, they remain and keep coming back, inescapably. Just as real and profound are the anxieties of millions of mentally ill and clinically isolated. But anxieties about atomic waste, overpopulation, mass starvation, etc.? No. There is no real anxiety about our collective fate. There is worry, political conscience, at the most, despair, always only the reflection through our own minds of something essentially abstract. On an individual's horizon of feeling, what can a mass death possibly be? Nothing, at most a shrug of the shoulders (or even: a secret sense of security, that an all too personal trail of sorrow has been abbreviated and come to an end). It may be that sometime before the turn of the first millennium there really was such a thing as an epidemic of anxiety, a mass psychosis, which was able to spread through the hot medium of religion. Then, damnation had a personal countenance. Anyone who believed in hell knew its tortures. But today, is our anxiety about the future anywhere near great enough to determine how we arrange our houses? It doesn't appear to be so, despite economic shock and all sorts of public demonstrations. In truth, we are so attuned to the present that it borders on being a curse.

But anxiety remained in their core. As before, horror only has an *I*, and it strikes those who are alone and sense a threat from something stronger, be it a boss, a father, illness or love, crowds, separation, accident, the fall.

Contrary to the many signs of a real threat, ours is less an "Age of Anxiety" than that of thirty years ago. Everything around us is organized in such a way that most of us succeed in leading an existence (to use a few words from Thomas Bernhard) that is a perfect distraction from existence.

. . .

The film *The Wooden Shoe Tree*, which depicts the life of the Bergamesk farmers in a compassionate though bitter way, invited the viewer to ask a sentimental question: Within the foreseeable future, will there ever be anything said about us – bogged down as we are in our bourgeois culture – that is kind, and that will preserve a similarly respectful memory? We don't really have a very strong sense of ourselves any more, and have become used to saying only ugly, ironic, and critical things about ourselves, we are ready to give up our heritage at the drop of a hat, as if we had had none at all, and certainly nothing that might be considered a loss, if at some time in the future our customs, our movements, our faces, our worries and happinesses were to be remembered. Would it really be only the archivist of destruction who could do justice to our gray-zone race?

. . .

Always in danger of completely losing all aesthetic decency – no matter how remote each of us holds his own – at the thought of cruise missiles, neutron bombs and similar equipment in front of my door, which could only serve to defend the thesis that highly civilized populations have the tendency to destroy themselves. "In any case, everything we do is entirely vain and ridiculous" – this originally religious perception of futility, in worship of God and the stars, occasionally seems very secular and near. Depending upon which compression waves are currently emanating from the threat. *The bomb* has already been here for some time, in place, ready to launch. Most of the time we never think about it. No human being can run around continuously with this breach of humanity in his head. But the threat is total, and, as such, like the "awful whole," is always present, can never be thought out of existence, but neither can it be thought. Its absurd weight will immediately crush whatever awareness we might gain of it. Still, it would be wrong, merely attempting to protect ourselves from stupidity, to ignore the relevance of a continuing existence for our common endeavors, and often, suddenly, for our entirely subjective definition of sense, and turn solely to political protest (which, in the case of the neutron bomb, was actually somewhat useful, at least to begin with). The place where all of the warheads are located is a very special one; in our reality we hardly know of another place where factual reality and a paranoid system of mania overlap to such a degree. Where is the real structural difference when the paranoid *I* feels itself, without exception, hunted and threatened by the "entirety" of the rest of the world, and when the biological life on the planet *really* is totally threatened by an entirety of extermination? Today, it is no longer a dialectical game to view the delusions of a paranoid as the inner reflection of our actual situation. The totality is not only the false, bad entirety of the thinker, not only a psychotic syndrome, it has also taken on real physical form: the potential Mega-End as the dully erect potential, hunched down in its underground silos, its "Rheingold"-forge, launch-ready at any moment, and subject only to the vicissitudes of power.

Si vis pacem, para bellum. If you want real peace, graveyard peace, the peace of ruins, then arm for war. Deterrence has been bought for the price of *limitless* terror in the heart of everyman, and perhaps for the price of destroying our own emotional defenses, our economy, our society. The threat may often escape our consciousness, but probably not our unconscious. To a large extent, our consciousness protects itself with a diversion from this threat which is equivalent and total. Today, we even view the brilliant photographs of the devastation of Hiroshima with aesthetic gain, photogenic catastrophe in magazines, a whiff of the romanticism of atomic ruin, nothing is real, our nation is even processing historical feelings of guilt in the psychology lab of a TV series. Maybe we have the unreality of our media civilization, this river of forgetting that girdles the world, this careful separation of humankind from humanity, with one word – television – to thank for the fact that we are still alive at all!

But it isn't only we few, the artistically critical in want of an art, who have been forced to confront this view of the unreal situation of mankind, is it?

Isn't there anyone in some citizens' action group, for example, be its goal nothing more than the relocation of a traffic light, who feels that he is at the focal point of real action? Of course! But this tiny focal point of action is itself a will-o'-the-wisp of reality, vanished *in toto*, unfathomable, always threatening out of the dark to overwhelm, causing the conventional, and maybe even every other kind of capacity for political judgment to fail.

Now and then, all political endeavor looks cute when seen against the backdrop of the high waves, the intensities, of real events. We are experiencing phases of world politics in which we can hardly any longer believe in the existence of the political, but only in the power of a world death wish that through national and economic conflicts creates the most foolish of rationales, and that has long been operating independently of what the great powers actually seek and are able to do. When we talk about a *lust* for war, we must assume that this death urge, bound up with libido, has developed into a gigantic masochistic horniness which the human race no longer knows how to contain. In the meantime, the so-called limited conflicts offer no guarantees that they will remain limited, and see to it that there is only a limited discharge of destructive energy. All too quickly an agglomeration of events emerges, aiming at the entirety and striving toward a state of "eternal détente." The current situation of heightened excitability and weakness is, among other things, the consequence of an atomic strategy that for decades has, with impulses of intimidation, scare tactics, and threats, been able to wear down and blight the natural will of the race to survive. And it is being further weakened as the earth has become unsafe under our feet, and we see its energy-giving resources running dry. This second fierce, greedy negativism rules in a world economy, entered upon a course, which can hardly be corrected, to manage to its end every resource we have, and this at breakneck speed. Quick, quick, are the words they use, why hesitate and restrict? Let's live it up, show off again, set everything on fire and blaze brightly. Let's get it all behind us!

In the last ten years, we have seen how the subjective health and behavior of the individual has become more and more bound up with the endangered planet as a whole. All of a sudden, led by global analyses of ecology and energy policy, expansive words like *man, the earth, humanity* were imbued with a credible, existential-political content, while previously we were accustomed only to speaking about people within the most limited definitions of class. Subjective identification no longer referred to a revolutionary people of the Third World, nor to a closed knowledge culture (such as Marxist culture), nor to the circle of militant criticism of our own social order; none of these realms, which are basically concerned with the requirements for a better, i.e., freer, life, offered an answer to the question of naked survival itself. Despite, or just in the midst of, all these currents, movements, and solidarities that are now spreading, in the end (again) it will be the individual alone who must find the answer. An individual who is more than the ensemble of his social circumstances; this overaged, highly developed, continuously disintegrating system of emotional, ritual, moral, informational and communication facilities, along with the precautionary arrangements of self-deception, indifference, diversion and blind zeal. Once everything is said and done, there is only you and the warheads, face to face. Though collective death, mega-suicide (the idea!) may sometimes even provide some sense of consolation, as long as it rules by threat it will torment every individual, even the ones who are always thinking: "I don't give it a thought," with episodes of emptiness and a ghastly crippling of consciousness. And everyone will be, no matter what he does while cultivating his circles, pursuing his goals, subject for some moments to that *brain over the earth* that comes surging out of the atomic cloud.

. . .

In ever widening circles of memory, our getting older continually revolves around our singular place of birth, German National Socialism. The interval is getting larger, but we can never break out of our concentric destiny. For those who emerged out of the excess of the century, there will be no phase of their lives in which they will not once more relate to this genesis, so that it actually forms the secret center, indeed the prison of all their intellectual (and emotional) endeavors. Occasionally, desperate attempts are made to rebel against the connection, occasionally it seems itself to mature, become more sovereign, more relaxed. What hasn't been tried in the realm of art alone to give our historical feelings truthful expression; it ranges from expressionistic bombast to psychoanalytical metamorphotic, from docudrama to obscene musical. A true solution, a being-able-to-free-oneself, has not been achieved. Only the death of history itself can free us, only the elimination of memory through the total presence of mass media, in which everything is only appearance, only aesthetic passing by.

In one point especially, we are, just like true Germans, filled with a kind of Faustian drive to study, to find out not what held the world, but what once held the Germans together in their innermost beings. But we will never be able to answer this clearly enough, and consequently we will keep changing the way we ask our questions. Judgments that change with our own life experiences, and the perception of something we cannot simply call hell; of something that always evades us, at one moment within the borders of intimate connectedness, and, at the next, in demonic inaccessibility – this memory, unmollified a life long, seems to be claiming a modest decency for itself, no matter what form of *mastering* the past it confronts.

. . .

What is missing today, the national affirmative, we had then as a quack. But how far did the charisma of the Führer actually reach? Did he heal even one soul? Dumb question. The healing took place because the individual soul did not perceive itself. (The fanatic National Socialist, one of my own relatives I remember from childhood, was thought of as "the crazy woman" after the war. But she, the healthiest, the most stable . . .)

. . .

In the end, it sometimes seems as if all motion we can still carry out, even the most radical and fantastic, belongs to the inescapable working up and working off of that motion of terror, a sequence that the generation before us once carried out. We feel ourselves caught and locked up in the field of force of our parents' past, and maneuver as we may within these confines, with a repulsion so violent or a homesickness so perverse and wanton: all of our reaching has nothing to do with one *particular* motion – the hand to the gate!

. . .

When Aeneas, hero of Troy, landed in the harbor at Carthage, he discovered scenes of the legendary war he had just left behind him, carved into the marble of a temple, and among the warriors his own image.

A., only a party member, a fellow traveler in the Nazi Regime, is sitting, now as an old man, near the front row in a movie theater, and suddenly in an old newsreel or a Hitler documentary, he recognizes himself among the shouting crowds, sees himself, the roaring young man in a close-up. Yes, he thinks, and feels himself anonymous right down through his fingertips, I was there, I yelled, I was one *Volk* – one cry. Now I am sitting alone among a crowd of young people in a dark movie theater, nothing but critical heads who can only wonder about all those screams, who even break out into howling laughter and have no respect at all for evil.

. . .

On a walk through the Tiergarten. Frost and sun. Ducks on the icy banks of the Landwehr canal. Ice skaters on the small lake. The old Spanish Embassy with the gloomy pomp of an old ruin. At the back of the building, like the imprint of a fossil, the walled-up vault of a chapel, a stone crucifix. Silence, empty castle of Fascism behind an overgrown garden. Even the excess of the century is aging toward a forlorn Romanticism.

Nevertheless: keep everything, preserve! Do not tear down!

The judge asks the old man, the camp guard Fuchs, what he thinks about the extermination of the Jews today. The man with heart illness answers according to the model of the unteachable: "The Jews should have been deported to a deserted island." The judge: "And what would you say if the State ordered all people named Fuchs to be deported to a deserted island?" Fuchs, subdued: "The Jewish Question should have been solved in a proper manner." The pedagogical judge: "What do you mean by proper?" The Nazi, thus driven into a corner, finally, very quietly, says what we want to hear: "The Jews should have been left in peace."

. . .

Liberation from conventional forms of political thinking is what the ecologists are calling for; even the supplanting of political ways of life by new anarchic forms, integration of the Free Zones into a Free State, the naive and the analytical are joined in common cause here, everyone's eyes are directed toward the perennial (rather than the utopian) and we even suppose that in the end only a world government can preserve existence. In his book *Society against the State,* the French anthropologist Pierre Clastres describes the song of the Guayaki Indians as a primitive, metapolitical need of mankind to free itself from the constraints of a trading society. A singing man exists for himself, he is free of his social role. The language, the song – the model of the communications universe is also, itself, the means to escape it. "If man truly is a 'sick being,' then it is because he is not only a 'political being,' and because his greatest wish derives from his restlessness, the wish to escape a necessity which is hardly be accepted as fate, and shed the demands of trading, to reject his social being in order to emancipate himself from his *condition.*"

. . .

The simple, swift song, subsidiary theme in the opening movement of Mendelssohn's Octet; so gentle, sociably unified; happily attending; nebulously upwards and forwards, and if only in wonderful greeting! The unifying ancillary whisperingly given. Only music can speak of heavenly companionship.

. . .

Wittgenstein (*Philosophical Investigations*): "In school, children learn that 2 x 2 = 4, but not that 2 = 2."

Meanwhile, in real life, we must see the so-called identity problem more in terms of what is known in the natural sciences and logic as a "solved problem." The identity we are *seeking* does not exist. Apart from a few external, official attributes, there is nothing which would speak for the existence of the individual as an organized whole. Not even the body is unitary and at one with itself. As rarely as opinions, are the steps of our feet unchangeable; they are a means of expression, very variable; and even the circulation of our blood displays itself, changing gestures and style to the extent that it reacts to life habits, encounters, and work. From the standpoint of a boundless psychosomatics, every organ says one thing today, and another tomorrow. This *I,* deprived of every transcendental "extrinsic" definition, exists today only as an open partitioning in a torrent of countless systems, functions, findings, reflexes, and influences, exists on so many different levels of scientific and theoretical nomenclatures, in so many "discourses," plausible in themselves, that by comparison every system of logic and psycho-logic of the one and individual appears absurd. The totally here and now exposes its pluralistic chaos. It is an abundance of extracted movements that do not fit together, an abundance of microscopic details from entirely different models of perception, in which we can barely infer what is real. Under such conditions, to make inquiries about the self leads us into the schema of a mad man who feels he is being populated by "alien beings" and disintegrating.

In the face of this dilemma it is good to know: there is this 2 = 2, it can be thought, it can be expressed. But this is not you, you are not an identity. Of course, you are more than a mere ensemble of laws and structures. Closed in the back, to the front you are an open-end creature. And that is why it is good to understand, from childhood on, the meaning of addition without a sum, or to learn the addition of the unsum.

Of course, we wish each of the countless desperate identity seekers who are struggling to find the way to themselves, we wish that they may finally imagine they have found it, their "identity," be it in the community, in work, in the political, or whatever other adventure of their existence. Here, we are obviously dealing with a foundered search for belief, in the same way we once struggled for "our God." Nevertheless, it hurts us every time we hear this ardent cliché of identity, the allusion to God, or rather the dissonance of self-deification, which the small, the free and wretched subject has presumed upon himself.

. . .

It is ridiculous to live without belief. Thus, in regard to one another we have become the most ridiculous creatures, and our best knowledge has not prevented us from assuming that we ourselves are the discharge of a divine roar of laughter.

. . .

God is of everything we are, we are eternally beginning, the wounded conclusion, the open end through which we are able to think and breathe.

. . .

No one who has proven himself in his primary situation, whether it be by earning money, or in a blind drive to do research, or through self-intoxicating reason, will be able to live without seeking refuge somewhere. He will need something higher than the peak of his freedom, under whose protection and in whose name he gathers the utmost of power. The more honorably he has proven himself, the stronger he will become through his urge for submission.

. . .

No one has been more deprived of their powers of perception, not by the church, not by war, than we who have been made dull through irradiation, we who still want to think and want to see can only do it in flash-fade, lonesome voyeurs whose world-vision is ruled by the jump cut, the way a slotted aperture makes a one-mark peep-show flicker. If Mörike had switched back and forth among six TV channels, always looking for something new!, run up and down the shortwave dial, he would never have been able to come up with a *developed* form. . . . Whoever is writing these days may try to artificially shut himself off, and make things different, but these remain the true conditions under which he will write. The stamina of fashion, of views, of ecstasies, and how it's accelerating, how it's overlapping, hopelessly the wishful being stands there in the face of obsession and undertow, once more to seize from rushing mists a *form*, worth all longing. . . . But no, behind the clock current is the blood-trace of forgetting, fading: there where the head of being rears up unfathomably, gazes fiercely and dives again, everything ours is still there.

I don't know what memory is. It's even come to the point where my sentences start to waver when a verb is supposed to be in the past tense. But don't we need memory for the health of the entire organism, the way we need dreams in our sleep?

And don't we also live to continually fill out memory? So that what has been will not be nothing, when one day every expectation will have disappeared and the broad sail of the journey is lying slack in the grass.

Punctured, torn to pieces even the last, dearest good: that which was.

. . .

Nietzsche's hatred of anti-Semitism: "So absurd, so unjustified, it is one of the sickest excesses of Imperial Germany's gawking self-scrutiny." In the meantime we have become adequately familiar with the gawking self-scrutiny of Federal Germany, too, and we know that the more critical the issues of economic prosperity, the more vain this scrutiny becomes, and that consequently the hostile feelings toward the too many foreigners in our county will begin to grow again. Of course, in the rest of Europe, in France and England as well, there will be, in part even more violent, but also more open protest against the influx of foreign workers; but no matter what economic justification such needs for self defense may have, in this country, in no time, they truly will merge with the well-known and long empty teats of racist passions. When we notice the sudden increase in hate, which is no less common among young people than it is among the old, proven racists, we might get the impression that German emotional life has for some time essentially consisted of a gap; nothing of the colorful mélange that came about could fill it, nothing stirred; once xenophobia appears we immediately sense: Attention! The feeling is feeling again, it has come to possess something central again.

"I don't want to know how many Turks were there," says the Berlin housewife, in the morning at the Edeka shop, after there had been sit-ins during the night, shop windows were broken, and looting began. (Of course, among others, the glass window panes of the Kreuzberg Turkish quarter did not escape the unrest intact). Apparently, we have now again named the ethnic scapegoat responsible for all the problems in our own society, and at this rate we won't have to wait much longer for the conspiracy theories to start popping up again, too. But now there are still a thousand prescribed sensitivities, in the mass media moral tremors (like *Holocaust*) punctually faded-in, and just as punctually, after a generous period of time, we are served the emotionally pornographic amusement of Nazi musicals and costume film nostalgia. A sheer, inescapable, profound dishonesty and non-freedom pervades what is referred to as overcoming the past, the half enlightenment and the half glorification of the national, the German underground in each of us; this miserable ambivalence, these inner reparations costs which will never be paid off, could altogether, in connection with a real deterioration in living conditions, lead very quickly to a situation where the crooked German soul rises up furiously, and simply shakes off the indigestible ballast, the illusion of irredeemable guilt, and cures itself of evil by wanting and doing evil all over again. And it has already begun by spraying its poison over the foreigners in our country. In any case, it is not the moment in which we can safely trust that a liberal democracy, with its simple edge/middle thinking, will over the long term be able to manage the parapolitical and negativist needs of a nation. And the long term is no longer long. We should be prepared for a future in which abrupt events will take place at a much faster pace than over the past thirty years, in which repressed currents can accumulate and burst forth, and that very suddenly, without run-up, the safeguards of modern rationalism could simply "blow their circuits."

. . .

Without getting involved with culturally invalid comparisons, we must conclude that the Iranian Revolution and its consequences brought about a much greater change in the atmosphere of world politics than anyone might have at first thought possible. A teaching came over to us (uprooted) from the East that although the "wheel of history" cannot be stopped or rolled back, there are very stable human forms of existence in which the "wheel of history" itself plays a completely subordinate role. And this teaching was given to us at precisely that moment when our culture, along with its command system of economic overdevelopment and overabundance, has fallen into an acute crisis of historical definition. Therefore we received – with the special signal of Americans being taken hostage – a profound warning from the pages of the daily political news: there are great epochs in the history of mankind (and possibly great epochs ready for rebirth) that in consistency, duration, tradition, plane, simplicity, and anti-materialism differentiate themselves from everything the dynamic of the Industrial Age has been hammering into us as a concept of history since the French Revolution. If the ascent of our history is completed at precisely the point where the ice of the recent past and progress is thinnest, then, this is probably due, above all, to its connection with the spiritual traditions of Islam. In no way were these events isolated from the rest of the world, nor was the Islamic revolution isolated from the rest of the world. Rather, the burglary in the Gulf Region created a vacuum of predictability in the conventional game of the World Powers, and this has heightened the level of nervousness on both sides, and had as its consequence both the invasion of Afghanistan as well as the strengthening of anti-liberal forces in the U.S.A. The East/West strategies were severely disrupted by a small power swerving out of time, committed to a Holy War, and threatening, in the case of aggression, to set its own oilfields on fire.

. . .

It would be surprising, but no longer unthinkable, if one day in the distant future, from out of another time, the German Third Reich were no longer judged mainly on the basis of the bloody sense of form with which it disposed of the horrors of diffusion in the first Age of Masses, but rather would be remembered as the first quake to send everything into aberration, the First Jolt before the slowly powerful launch into a "historyless," static epoch.

. . .

The fruitlessly dialectical and conciliatory nature of Both-And, the schoolroom Marxist justification of something like Stendhal's subjectivism in the foreword to an East German edition of his journals ("went through analysis only to be able to better analyze his milieu") – by now, that is the glue and goo even in the thinking of our enlightened educational institutions, which no longer allow anything new to be recognized or to develop, which glue everything together with everything else, that is the sleepy, soothing reflection which makes learning the concept more important than an alert grasp for the unexpected.

Before we believe in the existence of intelligent life outside our own planet, we should be convinced of the existence of revolutionary ideas outside our own dominant establishment consciousness. Might not all sorts of things have surfaced over this past decade, living out their astonishing essence in the ether of our days, while we, owing to the dogmas and limits of our perception, did not even notice them, were not able to notice. The "suddenness" with which the ecological question took center stage is a more recent example of this. The objective obstructions and blind spots of our cognitive systems, as investigated by Bachelard and Foucault in the history of natural science, come to mind when we recall how amazingly late the panic-induced birth of our energy debate was. Without a doubt, long before the report of the Club of Rome appeared, long before car-free Sundays, we knew about environmental pollution, the threat of shortages of vital resources, the limits of growth, in general; we had done the research, written and published. But even if this knowledge had been broadcast over all the television channels of the world, the thinking, specifically the critical thinking at the height of the so-called technological revolution, would simply not have accepted this knowledge, would have blanked it out. The rupture – the "shock" – hit at the sight of one symbol: the main arteries of communication desolate and deserted, lifeless roadways on car-free Sunday. (The prohibition was, after all, quite sensible, even if not for the stated reasons of energy conservation. It owed its implementation to nothing but the panicked confusion of a politics clobbered by the bright light of day, which in terms of the future had suddenly realized that it was wrong, from the ground up; which recognized that it would remain irretrievably wrong, and, given its false dependencies as well as its false self-assurance, would become even significantly more damaging as long as it did not solve itself, and that is what it would have to do, not in order to make room for someone else's politics, or another politics, but openly to admit that there is no politics *for* human beings, that the rulers in the East and the West have as much interest in the survival of mankind as do the computers of their respective secret services: namely, none at all.)

· · ·

What impenetrable lameness keeps coming at us from the stage into our hearts and heads! What crazy, helpless and insolent ways of handling "reality" are devastating our theaters! We need someone who speaks an entirely different language. Someone who comes to us from a well thought-out distance, who comes to us from somewhere far beyond the continents of art we know, and really seeks something in the theater which cannot be found anywhere else. A pirate after many long years of endless searching for treasure, in vain everywhere in reality, and the theater is the last shore he is heading for, his last hope, in whose environs his inner voice suddenly shouts: "Hot! . . . Hotter! . . ." and he is circling the hiding place, the certain treasure closer and closer, coming closer and closer to him . . . and the treasure he lifts up is so much its own substance that it is able to exist proudly, shining and shimmering next to acknowledged reality. He says: "I was seeking something which could not be found among men."

. . .

May it not be the Aha! of something resolved and revealed we hear escaping humans and audiences, but rather the Ha! – astonished at having snatched a tiny essentialness.

. . .

For me, an interest in people in the splendor of their everydayness, awakened through the actor's labor, reaches its high point in a comedy like *Husbands*, a film by Cassavetes. This is the best, in the most fortunate of circumstances, our sort can hope to attain using our own means: it has already been achieved. Seduction through the actors' art, which I have never escaped; an illogical being in love with people who *show* what is going on inside of them – it happens here in a friendly realm of males and masculine sensitivity. From here we must look outward for something else. Beyond this realm there is certainly another art (even for the actor). An art which denies itself the delights of perfect normality, and once more turns to the intricate demands of the symbolic; even when running the danger that what is created might only be able to celebrate the *idea*, which is no longer within his reach as the basis for characterization.

. . .

The difficulty working on drama, which should after all draw us into great conflicts and falls from great heights, which we would otherwise have no occasion to experience: these days, such conflicts and antitheses cannot even be argued within the realm of thought. The world of our experience is full of ambivalence and double bonding, full of a material "diversity of opinion" and of a terribly mediocre quid pro quo. This allows the sheer opposition of two contradictory positions in the theater to become an extremely artificial and unreal confrontation. But in precisely this, if it were to succeed, the age-old paradigm of the theater would be sufficiently well-served; for what really matters is proving that the models of the theater are older, stronger and more capable of surviving than anything we might bring to them from our present.

. . .

I believe it is right to expect that works of art, especially films, will continuously engage us in moral evaluation, and this in a sequence which causes our judgment to rollercoaster up and down, so that we find ourselves with no way out of a hot-and-cold bath of sympathy and censure, of good and evil, or whatever terms we may variably employ to appraise one and the same person. Genet once depicted the sexual aspect of political morals, their transvestite core, the strong homosexual character of opposites. Melville, the film director, followed him in the same vein with colder figures of veiled idolatry and American male love. We loathe the *flic* (in the movie of the same name) when he beats his devoted stool pigeon, a lovely transvestite, and wrongfully accuses him of betrayal. At the same time, we cannot get the policeman's melancholy face out of our minds; he remains the central figure, Alain Delon, the hero. And it is his own transvestite affiliation with a criminal gang he must fight, which lends him the necessary heroic solitude in our eyes. He has distanced himself from his office, has already worked his way so far into the other camp that we must question whether or not, at the decisive moment, he will still be capable of leaping into action playing his cop's role. And in fact, at the end of the film, we are confronted with a cruel surprise that threatens to almost completely disqualify our hero, if it were not for his unimpeachable type, who through offense and guilt gains in silent stature and respect for a sufferer. The *flic* finally catches up with the crook in front of the Hotel Splendid at the Arc de

Triomphe – the fugitive moves to draw, but he doesn't even have a weapon, and the policeman, Delon, immediately shoots him down. In the end, the petty little criminal showed himself to be as courageous as a samurai and took revenge on his great enemy, our hero, by forcing him back into the role of a brutal cop, and turning him into a cowardly murderer. He pins his death on Delon – and just the same thing happens at the end of Stroheim's *Greed*, when at the last moment the victim handcuffs his murderer and condemns him to dragging the corpse of his victim across Death Valley.

Similar reversals of judgment when first attempting to understand certain events of political terrorism. To begin with, a dead Holger Meins himself became a hero for the merely sympathetic and uninvolved TV-citizen; but his Genet partner, the Presiding Judge of Superior Court, who shortly thereafter was murdered in an act of revenge, was for his part then able to book a sudden innocence, became a victim himself, thus encroaching on the honor of the slain hero of anarchy. The passive viewer-contemporary obviously develops an enhanced need to occupy himself with secret shifts in attitude. Even yesterday, his heart pounded for the convicted, cowering, humiliated child murderer, because on television, of course, he saw how this man was being cruelly insulted and humiliated by the crowds standing around the court building. Today, his heart pounds against another, not yet convicted murderer who stabbed the family of a bank director, along with all his children. Because of an overabundance in the supply of identification options, he would long since, if he were an individual of the old sort, have become schizophrenic; through the absurd waste of his sympathy for the most disparate of parties he would have to have long since become indifferent and numbed. But he is no longer an individual of the old sort. The recklessness of passive emotions corresponds to the heart's own dominion of ambivalence, thoughtless, no longer confined by custom or external forces. And we continuously expose even our closest friends, and our nearest, to entirely conflicting assessment, and in forming our most intimate judgments we display neither discipline nor constancy. We may even add the paradoxical assertion that at present it is almost impossible to keep a relationship alive without – as openly as possible, as directly as possible – surrendering ourselves to the variability of our feelings, being aware of them and thus entangling ourselves in them right up to the very brink of strangulation. Our emotional lives have become the absolute regents of our social and personal relationships; in this role it will most probably be overburdened and thus bring about its own bankruptcy.

. . .

What are we to think of sayings like: "Everything which can be clearly thought, can be clearly expressed in every language"? (Marcuse said this in one of his last interviews, in answer to the question of whether or not he had ever missed the German language in California; but every German teacher makes similar claims.) Still, how can fading, multi-branched codes of the unconscious be *clearly* expressed, if language is to keep from distorting these messages? As far as this is concerned, Lacan listened a good deal more profoundly than Freud had. What is to be said is infinitely long. And actually, it cannot be organized according to the rules of grammar or common sense. To organize means to take the body, the anatomy, to be the measure of all things, the measure of language, above all. In the meantime, the unconscious that speaks is *also* a mass, a stump, is rain, decay and wind.

So let's leave the impudent demand for clarity aside. Let's make do without a pathetic delight in paradoxes, intricate clevernesses and similar sorts of light in the spray of the maelstrom. Everything which has been brought "to a point" is so small, the expressible in the purity of its thought.

. . .

Neurotic obsession with clear thinking. A man must wash out his brain lobes several times a day. And see in every clear sentence that comes out: how painful it is to do without the filthy-essential of all his life's tumors. Become much more nonsensical. All further understanding will be turbulent.

. . .

Overnight the cherry tree completely lost its robe of blossoms. It is lying there worn out, a piece of dirty wash on the ground. When we want to admire nature, we use facile expressions like: Nothing is more disgusting to me than the idea of a better world. Only because in the meantime the so-called utopian has become the property of people too lazy to think. Only because we have come to understand how many bloody remnants of murdered existence have been swept under this flying carpet. But it will do the desperate little good to make themselves nature's favorites.

It is certainly true, that on the one hand we want to tear down the scaffolding of repression everywhere, but on the other, to watch from our houses in devoted silence as the treetops murmur, and this forever. It is also certainly true that in the end we will always alternate between uprising and settling, between East and West, between sorrow and emptiness, and never be able to make a clear choice without doing significant damage to ourselves.

. . .

Be nothing, nothing but simple gesture, which the listener fills in. Hollow gesture.

. . .

Cioran: "The experience of the horrible, which alone can give our words a certain gravity . . ." Yes, and we can give an example of that: the way the words move closer together in order to resist the threat from the unsayable.

. . .

In response to an outrageous question, just look straight at someone, don't evade, don't answer. Not being able to answer, but not saying so, and not explaining why.

. . .

Desire undermines the foundations of life: melancholy and accumulation.

. . .

Homer calls the fragile sound of the voice of the shadow of death a *trizein* – a twitter, a chirp. We are reminded of this when we walk through the streets and hear the high whistle of television picture tubes behind windows.

. . .

For Cioran, God and angel and devil are no more than thought samples in order to compare them with man. "The angel's misadventure," he says, "comes about because he never has to try hard to gain glory." But glory is not really a problem for an angel.

Cioran takes the Holy to be nothing more than the suprahuman, seeing in it the better, higher conditions of human being fulfilled. Here, the philosopher is thinking like a child who calls an angel down without a shudder. The earth is peopled equally by angels, devils and gods. We are probably not alone. At least descendants of heavenly and infernal hordes cross through our breasts and our polity. And isn't it possible that we will soon be seized by a new allegorical desire? A desire for grand incarnation, for becoming the flesh of the many dreamed-out ideas of our century. We cannot think so much and stretch out so abstractly as we have done in the age of science, without in the end having something Entire, One Skin, a new body out of an idea, out of mist and light, arch toward us . . . the wondrous ass of psychoanalysis, the breasts of social justice, the crossed legs of the economy and ecology, the eyes of the biologist, the arms of the fall.

. . .

By inventing and building the machines of integrated circuits, computers, data banks, super storage – weren't we being secretly guided by the idea that the decisive cultural achievement of our age would have to consist of adding up sums, creating an immeasurably large collection, a meta-archive, a giant memory of human knowledge, so that we ourselves could, at the same time, take leave of it, and lose our subjective involvement in it?

Basically, the idea of a computer is one of storage, of stockpiling and summary, and as such it seems to be accompanying the displacement of the previous era of progress and expansion. Above all, the electronic brain seeks to branch out along the surface of what already exists, it is not itself a manufacturing machine, but operates in the service of control, and the uninterrupted control of technical production as well as social processes.

. . .

In the beginning, microelectronic circuits basically represented a simplified (partial) emulation of human brain function, and in certain capabilities surpass their performance by far, for example in the speed with which they can carry out complex computations. Since his appearance thirty thousand years ago, man has always felt the need to invent something that surpassed the attributes he naturally possessed, but at the same time had to learn that these better things set him back; just as industrial machines set human hands back, and over the long run will lead to atrophy of the organ (and for the time being only suggested in clumsiness, in psychosocial shyness: not knowing what to do with your hands . . .) Given this, we must assume that in the areas where the memory machine has achieved perfection, it will set us back as well, and will promote the regression of our ability to remember. It is insane to assume that an organ relieved of its hard work will therefore be better and healthier, and can therefore better concentrate on a "statement of fundamental questions." Basically our memories know nothing superfluous. The abundance and wealth of divergent operations and information are the actual *movement* that generates its energy, and even the hard number work is not done in vain; everything we do ourselves multiplies, activates, and strengthens our memory. Only the total consumer does not remember. That machine, which in parts represents an emptying of the human brain, may possibly lead more quickly to its atrophy than those machines which eased the body's physical burdens, contributed to specific illnesses of the organs and the soul. (For the present, the last available site of subjective production will be illness.) The big machines of our century: the car, the television, the computer, at the very outset, *deprived* humans of something (as Ernst Jünger observed early on when he first caught sight of car drivers) – the numbness in the visage of the total consumer, the numbness in the visage of those who no longer fantasize, of the television viewers who no longer remember in the face of the monstrous archive of the ubiquitous present, in the face of the true terminal of cultural memory: the end of the line for sensual perception. In the narcissistic attention which a maker dedicates to his product, in love with his apparent likeness, the computer molds its temporary, static, restricted kind of intelligence back into the human mind.

The passive, over-informed consciousness, no longer able to produce wish, idea, memory, experiences instead a (otherwise only known to madness) synchronicity of incompatibles and *thinks* up a data salad, indiscriminately, out of what was on hand. None of us will be spared this state any longer. How shocked we often are at the bizarre output of our own archive! Images out of a film by Glauber Rocha and words of Gotthold Ephraim Lessing. In them we seek to grasp the motive, the energy of the heterogeneous. It is pointless. It was only a useless game of a memory aping a machine. A cultural equality that assigns everything equal value, as phenomenon, is a wasteland of consciousness; and it is growing, it is pressing on toward the brink of idiotism: how vast is the world between Ezra Pound and Wim Thoelke?

An association apparently forever unknown and inexplicable; those things most remote from one another, in the perfect purity of their divergence; there is no way from this to that; only the confused microcircuits of a computer gone wild can establish such synchronicity, but no soul, no unconscious can do it.

(Apropos André Leroi-Gourhan, *Gesture and Speech*)

. . .

On the one hand: the quick thought about the "atrophy of the hand," the unbolting of the forehead, the acceleration of the entropy of knowledge – on the other hand: the inert mass of time of millennia in which the genetic destiny of mankind unfolds, unalterably, not to be accelerated; physical state and inherited patterns of behavior of homo sapiens since the early Stone Age, almost stationary. Deterioration of our common inheritance over the course of cultural evolution nearly irrelevant, since this is so fast that biological evolution remains – approximately 100,000 times slower – almost inoperative. Since Charlemagne, only forty generations have passed by. (Friedrich Cramer, *Progress through Renunciation*)

. . .

A person's generally formed concept of self is determined, now as before, by history, culture, and social achievement, and hardly at all by the progress of knowledge about his "nature." Today, in the so-called Age of Natural Sciences, things are not much different from the way they were before Darwin, before Freud. Beyond the workings of instincts and drives, our own bodies have not been a source of intellectual lesson.

Although our knowledge has long since progressed into the microspheres of human life, where the traditional image of homo sapiens is beginning to break up, the ideological concept of self is still struggling against an acceptance of the revolutionary achievements of its spirit, against taking them into consideration in the imagination, as it has done with the loss of religion or with the findings of psychoanalysis. Still, we are not dealing with tiny bits of interstellar matter, but with the fate of our own kind, a realm which we might expect to move the egocentric curiosity of the thinking subject. However, as far as our sense of the most elementary aspects of nature is concerned, we do not, for example, experience biological processes at the cellular level; they inform (except through malfunction or illness) neither the conscious nor the unconscious. Our innermost processes are controlled by the device, the bio-computer. And while we believe, struggle, cry, sleep, criticize, the enzymes intrepidly go about their work, diligent, understanding, indifferent. Liberated from his mirror image, a human being would be forced to see through himself, recognize himself as the prodigious creation of extrahuman forms and structures, leading him to always doubt his identity if he were forced to view his only authentic portrait, which is that of a transitional phenomenon, maybe only that of an aberration, a branch of mistletoe on the life tree of the earth. Only in a state of what is perhaps skittish, or maybe even mysterious quiescence could he experience the entire abundance of his "nature." It would be an experience similar to the neverending diversity of feelings which creates desire in motionlessness, and which finds its expression in the infinite variety of plant forms (Ponge). At our deepmost standstill, in a spiritual instant, we will incorporate into our consciousness the Form-Universe through which we live, and in it we will recognize nature's monstrous desire to overcome mankind.

. . .

"Purposeful mastery of reality," I hear a teacher say, that is what we must always keep encouraging our children, our youth, to seek. This is also why we must speak out against smoking hashish, because it makes people lazy and indifferent and hinders critical orientation within our surroundings. How regrettable these miserable, rundown convictions are that keep bubbling merrily out of the mouths of our educators! (The '68 generation, who again found good fortune, and who will now keep broadcasting their humble and clever thoughts, unalterably, from behind their comfortable professorships . . .) With such incantations – Mastering Reality! – hard-pressed reason attempts to transform the thicket of the living into an empty world of precepts, and this is the true irrationality. Their thin prayer, long since drowned out by the noise of the language drop-out, stakes its claims on the basis of status, and is all the more cramped and zealous, and our forsaken teachers repeat and repeat – we haven't learned anything else – the cold, emaciated vocabulary of critical comprehension that seems to become a touch more abstract with each repetition. What is: reality mastery, purposeful? How are we supposed to bring this about? If only they would come out and be honest, and say: everyone should do the best he can to get along as happily as he can without losing his mind and his self respect. Rather than a vibrant career, most of our lives will be more like an arduous rope climb, hand over hand. Everyone should, as best he can, help (with or without hashish) himself, and those who become close; together with others, try to cut a path through the forest and keep groping along until perhaps sometime, somewhere, a clearing will open, a river will appear, and – in the best case – a certain calm, far from indifference, will compensate us for our efforts at trailblazing.

. . .

But what will we, and our children, master when our three-dimensional sense for what is real has been marred and gradually eliminated? Through the media, according to Jean Baudrillard (all of the following quotes from his book *Symbolic Exchange and Death*) – "Overgrowth, through the media of the category of *faits divers*, of the political. . . . On television, merely by its presence, social control has come in to its own. . . . Even over the long term, the impossibility of police mega-systems means only that through feedback and self-direction the prevailing systems will integrate these mega-systems, as useless as they have now become, into themselves. That which they have negated, they are capable of incorporating as *additional variables*. They are the censors of their own operations; no meta-system necessary. . . . The street is the only existing anti-medium. . . . The age of the social, which ends like a dying star in a black hole – the implosive energy which follows from the boundless compression of the social, which reaches the state of a system in extreme control, an overloaded net of knowledge, information, power. . . . We cannot comprehend this force because our entire imagining is directed toward logic expanding systems.

"In the Paris hypermarket of culture, Beaubourg, the retotalizing of all distributed functions of the social body and life (work, leisure, media, culture) is taking place in homogeneous Time-Space; the retranscription of all contradictory currents in terms of integrated circuits; Time-Space of an absolutely rational simulation of social life . . ." The great event of this period, the great trauma is that agony of fixed referent, the agony of the real and rational with which the age of simulation is dawning. While so many generations, and especially the last, have lived history at full gallop, either from the euphoric or the catastrophic perspective of a revolution – today, we get the impression that history has pulled back into itself, leaving a fog of indifference behind it, criss-crossed by currents but emptied of all its referents. In this void, the phantasms of a sunken history flow together, the arsenal of events, ideologies and retro-modes assemble – not so much because people still believe in them, or still base any of their hopes on them, but simply to allow a time to revive in which history *at least* existed, in which power at least existed (and be it fascist power), or at least a risk of life or death existed. Everything is okay in order to escape this void, the leukemia of history and politics, this absolute of values – in wild confusion, according to the level of distress, all contents can be called up, all earlier history will be resuscitated in riotous disarray – no more compelling idea which would select, only nostalgia accumulating endlessly: war, Fascism, the pomp of the Belle Epoque, or revolutionary struggles, everything is equivalent and mingles randomly in the same morose and gloomy exaltation, the same retro-fascination.

. . .

Is survival really all we care about? Weren't we always looking for a better life? Baudrillard asks the ecologists somewhat bitterly. Yes, they answer, suddenly we're talking about naked survival. But how it comes to be at issue, that is also of some interest.

. . .

. . . to know all of this and to let this knowledge be, was one thing.

. . .

Venice, yearend, her back pressed to the locked Porta Sant'Alipio of the Church of San Marco, in order to resist the draw of looking back, which is one with the draw of the great square, almost empty at midnight. Around the windows of the New and Old Procuratian, a thousand round lights that can turn this most open place into a festive interior, into a dream hall . . . . Oh, my year! What is it that keeps pulling me back? Where to? . . . The people, the ones alone at this hour, have an unusual way of leaning forward into their walk, now too fast and then unnaturally slow. They are all walking in contemporary reticence, as if they had been sent out onto the great showplace of history where they can play no role. The usual protective space of movement, the characteristic proportion which the pedestrian forms with his surroundings, with houses and passersby, street and traffic, is canceled out, or at least disturbed. The square, the slight, almost animated anxiety of the square lends his step a strange and un-autonomous aura. In such a silent tremor of the present, the city withdraws itself from us as the splendid backdrop and grand stage that we happily admire, and a secret tear opens, maybe the only still passable entrance to the past. History lives! and we are its very small, uncertain, but welcome guests.

A strong, bright song is coming out of a narrow street near the Café Quadri. A young woman has stood up from her circle of friends and is singing to them, not Venetian but Russian songs. These are art songs, and the voice is a trained soprano. Called out of their forlornness, so to speak, the few people on the square make their way to the street and gather at the singer's back. She is singing into the street and not to please her friends, who are sitting on wooden benches and are perhaps voice students like her. As she now begins to feel an audience growing behind her, she doesn't make a fuss, but opens herself to us with a half turn of her body and lets her melancholy exultation carry out into the enormous hall of San Marco Square. The young woman is standing there in her lambskin coat, her hands in her pockets, her head up and tilted to one side, and out of her child's mouth, in a clouded breath, rise these pure tones which she loves above all else, which her mouth forms and caresses. She senses a feeling of satisfied happiness from all of the listeners; representing each of us, she abandoned herself to the vibrations of the place and the hour, which may well confuse our walk, but surely lure song out.

This happened in the immediate vicinity, only a few meters away from a spot where I had once already experienced another moment of knowing, as exalted as it was disjoined. Here, under the colonnades of Café Quadri in the summer of 1969, sat the sad illusion of an old man whom I had never met, and whom I admired like no other; there sat the famous philosopher, the round bald head I knew from photographs, the dark round eyes that seemed to be less animated by externals and visibles, by sculpturals, than by hearing, understanding, time-game. He sat alone, and left alone, at a table in the café in the middle of a wild stream of tourists, and I stared at him and I was sure it could only be him, the man from whom I had thought so much into myself. A little later I read in the newspaper that he had died during those summer days, maybe on the same day I had seen him in Venice, in a Swiss hospital.

Yes, a city of history, it is well known enough; and certainly for the simple reason that here we must look around us incomparably more astonished than anywhere else, and from this things unknown, invisible appear in us. If we spend a long time wandering through the streets, our senses and mind have almost too much to do, touch and feel forms, ornament, and signs of many times, pressed close, and they work together within the perimeter of a living, entirely real city (not in a museum). Our own Time-Dimension, unvarying and ground down by continually seeing bare concrete walls, is fiercely attacked and twitches along its surface, and imagination, even an enhanced, doubled vision, emerges out of its chinks.

. . .

The city of today essentially allows only us humans in. And it isolates us immediately. It separates us from those primary connections that rule our lives: the streets, cars, the buildings all of the same age, from all the dimensions, rhythms, and forms of our residential developments. Thus segregated, we are at first helpless, and nowhere near autonomous observers. Here, history looks back at us with its own beams and sometimes the surface of a cut stone X-rays us, an architrave scatters our minds right out to the skin of our dreams, an arch and then next to the stones, and just as solid as they are, an old augury pushed aside, shows itself to be a creature that does not exist.

. . .

I thank the young woman who stepped forward and did what is fitting for us all: gracefully lifted her head high into the foggy midnight sky in order to gather her breath for a song.